"I Hope You've Changed Your Mind About Not Telling Me About Myself, Corrado,"

Philippa said softly.

"No, I still think the best thing is for you to remember on your own."

"Please, Corrado, you must tell me. Am I . . . am I in love with you?"

He reached out swiftly and took her by the shoulders. "Philippa, listen to me. You've got to stop asking such questions."

"But I want to know the truth," she cried.

"And will you know it when you hear it?" He moved suddenly, drawing her close. "Yes," he murmured, "you're in love with me. You told me that it was only in my arms that you'd discovered what love meant."

He lowered his mouth until it touched hers, and at the feel of his lips on hers, her head swam until her own lips parted.

It was a tantalizing, bewitching, maddening, tormenting half kiss, both a warning and a demonstration of the power he was determined not to abuse.

"Well?" he demanded tensely. "Am I telling the truth, or am I lying to you, knowing that you can't tell the difference? *Did* you say you were in love with me?"

Dear Reader:

Welcome! You hold in your hand a Silhouette Desire—your ticket to a whole new world of reading pleasure.

A Silhouette Desire is a sensuous, contemporary romance about passions, problems and the ultimate power of love. It is about today's woman—intelligent, successful, giving—but it is also the story of a romance between two people who are strong enough to follow their own individual paths, yet strong enough to compromise, as well.

These books are written by, for and about every woman that you are—wife, mother, sister, lover, daughter, career woman. A Silhouette Desire heroine must face the same challenges, achieve the same successes, in her story as you do in your own life.

The Silhouette reader is not afraid to enjoy herself. She knows when to take things seriously and when to indulge in a fantasy world. With six books a month, Silhouette Desire strives to meet her many moods, but each book is always a compelling love story.

Make a commitment to romance—go wild with Silhouette Desire!

Best,

Isabel Swift
Senior Editor & Editorial Coordinator

Published by Silhouette Books New York
America's Publisher of Contemporary Romance

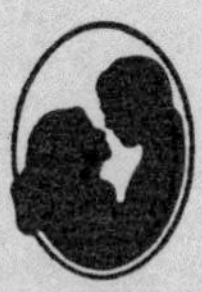

SILHOUETTE BOOKS
300 East 42nd St., New York, N.Y. 10017

ISBN: 0-373-05416-5

First Silhouette Books printing April 1988

America's Publisher of Contemporary Romance

Printed in the U.S.A.

Books by Lucy Gordon

Silhouette Romance

The Carrister Pride #306
Island of Dreams #353
Virtue and Vice #390
Once Upon a Time #420
A Pearl Beyond Price #503
Golden Boy #524

Silhouette Special Edition

Legacy of Fire #148
Enchantment in Venice #185

Silhouette Desire

Take All Myself #164
The Judgment of Paris #179
A Coldhearted Man #245
My Only Love, My Only Hate #317
A Fragile Beauty #333
Just Good Friends #363
Eagle's Prey #380
For Love Alone #416

LUCY GORDON

is English but is married to a Venetian. They met in Venice, fell in love the first evening and got engaged two days later. After fifteen years they're still happily married. For twelve years Lucy was writer on an English woman's magazine. She interviewed many of the world's most interesting men, including Warren Beatty, Richard Chamberlain, Roger Moore, Sir Alec Guinness and Sir John Gielgud. She also has camped out with lions in Africa and has had many other unusual experiences, which at times provide the backgrounds to her books.

To every thing there is a season, and a time to every purpose under the heaven: A time to be born, and a time to die;
a time to plant and a time to pluck up that which is planted.

—Ecclesiastes 3:1

One

The man's face filled her vision. He'd haunted her for a long time, appearing out of the mist that surrounded her, then fading only to reappear again, his dark eyes fixed on her, intent and full of bitterness.

He followed her and she ran away in fear, yet she was deeply drawn to him. At last she turned and pleaded for his forgiveness, though she had no idea what she'd done. He smiled and opened his arms, and she knew that all was forgiven. She reached out, but at the last moment he withdrew, saying that some wrongs could never be made right. She cried out her despair, and the sound of her own voice awoke her.

He was still there, standing back against a wall. She noticed him before the nurse who was hovering to one side of her bed and the middle-aged woman seated on the other. He was a tall, dark man, whose brilliant eyes, filled with the bitterness she remembered from the dream, were fixed on her.

"Philippa," the middle-aged woman was saying anxiously, "thank heavens you're awake."

She turned her aching head on the pillow to regard the plump, kindly face streaked with tears. "Philippa," the woman said tearfully, "why did you do it?"

"Do what?" she asked, her voice a dry whisper.

"Run away like that, and on your wedding day."

She tried to recall running away... where... from what? No memories came. The name Philippa meant nothing to her, nor did she know this weeping woman. Her eyes flickered toward the man, still standing apart, watching her silently. "How long have I been unconscious?" she asked.

"Twenty-four hours," the nurse said. "Your car went off the road. Two men found you nearby and naturally they brought you to Signor Bennoni's house."

"Why 'naturally'?"

Through her haze she was suddenly aware of tension. There was a brief, shocked silence before the nurse continued, "They recognized you as Signor Bennoni's wife."

Signor Bennoni's wife? But I don't know any man of that name. I don't even know my own name.

Her thoughts echoed wildly through her head, and she looked this way and that, desperately trying to find something or someone that she recognized. But she found nothing. She lay in a comfortably furnished room that she'd never seen before, and the people around her were strangers.

She raised her left hand far enough to look where a wedding ring should be. The hand was bare.

At once the man by the wall came forward and leaned over her. "All this can wait. You must sleep now," he said, his voice gentle but commanding.

Her body seemed to respond to that quiet firmness of its own accord, and blackness enveloped her once more. When she awoke again she was alone with the middle-aged woman. Her head had stopped aching and her mind felt clear, but inside there was still a vacuum. "I don't know who I am," she said as calmly as she could. "And I'm afraid I don't know you. Are you my mother?"

"Oh, no. I'm your Aunt Claire. Your mother died when you were two."

"Well, Aunt Claire, please tell me who I am, and where."

"This is Italy, near Naples. You came here to be married a few days ago."

She frowned, but nothing happened in her mind. "Can I have my purse, please?"

Aunt Claire brought it and helped her to sit up. Philippa found a small mirror in the purse and studied herself. She was pale and had an ugly bruise on her forehead, but even illness couldn't destroy the firm, beautifully molded lines of the face or the effect of the green eyes and glowing chestnut hair.

She discovered a British passport. The face in the picture was her own, but this time perfectly groomed, as though time and money had been devoted to creating the glamorous look. "According to this I'm twenty-three," she said. "I'm English and my name is Philippa Davison."

"Your father was Edward Davison, of Davison Electronics. He was a great man. He started that firm from nothing, but it was worth a fortune when he died a month ago. You were his only child."

"Do I have any other relatives but you?"

"Only your husband. He was standing by the wall when you awoke."

"You asked me how I could have done something. What did I do?"

"After the wedding we were having a party. You said you had a headache and went upstairs early. Later we couldn't find you. Then someone said he'd seen you race off in Corrado's car." Aunt Claire looked uncomfortable. "We found your wedding ring on the floor."

Philippa pressed a hand to her head, which was beginning to throb again with the effort of trying to remember. "But *why*?"

Aunt Claire shook her head. "Only you know that."

But I don't. I don't know why I married Corrado Bennoni, or why I fled from him on our wedding day.

"What is my husband like?" she asked urgently.

"My dear, I only met him a few days ago. You've known him barely a month yourself."

"A *month*?"

"You met him at your father's funeral."

Philippa stared. "I rushed into marriage with a man I'd known only a month?"

"Well, he's very good-looking. Maybe he swept you off your feet, then at the last minute you panicked."

It sounded reasonable. Philippa couldn't have said why the picture of herself in a panic lacked conviction.

"After all," Aunt Claire continued, "it was a great shock to everyone when you—"

She broke off hastily as the door opened and Corrado Bennoni himself appeared. As Aunt Claire had said, he was a very good-looking man in his early thirties, with the black hair and vivid features of a southern Italian. His face was lean with high cheekbones that gave it a look of austerity. But his full, generous mouth contradicted that impression.

He was casually dressed in slacks and shirt, with the sleeves pushed up, exposing his tanned skin. His arms were well muscled—the arms of a man accustomed to manual labor. But his hands provided another contrast. The long, sensitive fingers hinted at an artist.

A deep feminine instinct, beyond reason or memory, told Philippa that this was an intriguing man, full of subtleties and surprises. The woman who lived with him could spend her life reveling in the joys of discovery. And he was her husband.

Aunt Claire scuttled out of the room, leaving Philippa alone with the stranger that she'd married and then deserted within hours. His look was distant, reserved, and she wondered if he hated her for humiliating him on their wedding day. She tried to read the truth in his manner, but he was polite and wary. "Are you feeling better now?" he asked, seating himself.

"Yes, but I can't remember anything."

A strange look crossed his face. "Do you mean that literally?" he asked, watching her closely.

"Apart from my passport details, I know nothing about myself or my past." She laughed defiantly. "You could tell me I'm the man in the moon, and I'd believe you."

"And you don't know me, either?" he asked slowly.

On impulse Philippa reached forward and put her hands on his shoulders, holding him for a long, silent moment while she frantically searched his features. "As far as I know, I never saw you before today," she told him at last. "And yet . . . it seems that we're married."

After a moment's hesitation he said, "In a sense we are."

She released him. "What do you...? Oh, I see. You mean we'd had the wedding ceremony but nothing else."

"I mean more than that. In this part of Italy it's the custom to have two weddings, a civil ceremony in the town hall, followed by a church service the following day. Your...accident...occurred on the evening of the civil ceremony. Without the church service we're effectively half-married."

Philippa stared at him, eyes wide, as the implications dawned on her. "You understand?" Corrado asked. "We can either go forward and complete our marriage, or we can go back and have it annulled."

She clenched her hands. "Corrado, why was I running away from you?" she demanded desperately.

A withdrawn look settled over his face. "I can't tell you that."

"Can't or won't?"

"Can't," he said harshly. "I'm not a mind reader, Philippa, and you didn't tell me you were going. You just vanished and left me to discover your disappearance by chance."

"Didn't I leave a note?" she asked wildly.

"Nothing."

"Perhaps I had a message immediately beforehand."

"Nobody came to the house. The phone didn't ring, either. Besides, if you'd gone away for such a reason you'd hardly have removed your wedding ring."

"Then the answer must lie between us." He didn't answer, and her voice rose in a frantic attempt to pierce the cool barrier he was keeping between them. "You must know something. You *must*."

"Hush, don't upset yourself. I'm sorry I was angry." He took hold of her shoulders and pressed her gently back against the pillows. The movement showed her the broad gold band gleaming on his left hand. Philippa looked at it, then up into his face, so close to hers that she could feel his warm breath on her cheek. She was suddenly conscious of the rough hair of his arm against her bare skin and the unnerving sensation of excitement that it gave her. She glanced down and saw that she was wearing a silky nightgown that exposed the tops of her full breasts. His hand on her shoulder seemed dangerously close.

Blushing, she averted her face from him still further. He drew back abruptly, and she covered herself with the sheet. "It's not very appropriate for an invalid," he agreed wryly, "but when your aunt went through your things that was the most modest nightgown she could find."

It was a bride's garment, designed to entrance a man and lure him to remove it. It told Philippa that she'd desired her bridegroom and wanted him to find her equally desirable. But she would have known that even without this clue. Her flesh still tingled where he'd touched it, and the sensation seemed to spread out from there, running like wildfire across her skin. She felt the telltale warmth in her cheeks and was glad of the blankets that kept Corrado from seeing that her toes were curling.

She longed to ask him if they'd shared passion in the short time they'd known each other. Some instinct told her that they hadn't. Amnesia might make her forget herself, her father and everything in her past, but nothing on earth could make her forget lying in the arms of this dangerously attractive man.

She sought his eyes, hoping to find some hint of the answer, and flinched as she saw their expression. His guard had slipped, and she caught a glimpse of the anger and bitter, outraged pride that he could barely control. Then it was gone, so quickly that she might have imagined it, and his eyes were as blank and unrevealing as a shuttered house. "Corrado," she pleaded, "tell me about us. Why did we marry? What do we feel about each other?"

He was silent for a moment, then he spoke with obvious strain. "This isn't the time. You're still very weak. Besides, it's better for you to remember of your own accord."

"What does it matter whether I remember or you tell me?"

"Because, as you've just pointed out, I could tell you that you were the man in the moon, and you'd believe me."

"Should I distrust what you tell me, then?"

"I want you to trust me, Philippa," he said quietly. "And I think you'll trust me more if I don't plant ideas in your head."

"But suppose my memory doesn't come back?"

"Let's hope it does, because soon you must make a decision about our marriage. Now I want you to get some sleep. I've stayed too long."

She thought he was going to walk out at once, but at the last minute he came to lean over her. He brushed her lips lightly with his own, and Philippa had a wild urge to put her arms around his neck and draw him to her. Controlling her desire, she let out a soft sigh. Until she'd broken through Corrado's reserve, her pride forbade letting him see how much he affected her.

It was only after he'd closed the door behind him that Philippa realized she'd been speaking in fluent Italian.

Their talk had left her tense and weary. Sleep began to claim her again. Corrado's face was there behind her eyes, but this time it bore the expression it had worn when he asked her if she could really remember nothing. It was the look of a man making a swift and vital decision: to keep her in ignorance for his own purposes....

* * *

When she awoke she was alone. Her mind was still a blank, but she felt well enough to get out of bed and start examining her surroundings. She was in a large bedroom, furnished in a solid, traditional style. The bed was almost six feet wide, with a carved walnut headboard, and the rest of the furniture was in the same dark, attractive wood. The floor was parqueted and highly polished.

There were two paneled doors, one of which led to a small bathroom. Tall windows were hung with green curtains, and through them Philippa could see a sweep of beautiful countryside. The house stood high up, looking down over a huge bay with incredibly blue water. Across the bay in the distance were two mountain summits, very close together, their tops oddly flat. They dominated the surrounding countryside, looming, silent and mysterious, through the mist that swirled about them.

She turned and gazed into a long mirror near the windows. She was tall and slender with high, firm breasts. Pulling the nightgown against her, she splayed her fingers over her tiny waist, then the curve of her hips. She lifted the hem and surveyed long, slim legs, tapering to delicate ankles.

Her neck, also, was long, culminating in the firm lines of her jaw, and her chestnut hair fell in deep waves against her fair skin. Trying to be objective, she could see that the woman who gazed back at her possessed beauty and elegance. Was she being fanciful in detecting a touch of imperiousness about the set of her head and the angle at which she instinctively held her chin? If she'd met her reflection she would have thought that here was a person used to having her own way and who displayed determination and ingenuity in getting it.

She began opening the doors of her wardrobe. What she found inside made her eyes open wide in amazement. How could any woman need so much?

There were numerous items of all kinds and colors, and all of the very best quality. The names on the labels meant nothing to her, but her fingers sensed the fineness of the silk, wool, leather and corduroy. In the drawers she found lingerie of silk and satin finished with lace, in a variety of colors.

Her accessories were also the finest. There was a large variety, evidently to match her extensive wardrobe.

She turned out the contents of her purse and discovered a number of credit cards, money and makeup but no letters or photographs. Where the clues to her personal life should have been there was only a frightening blank.

She stared at all her luxurious possessions and wondered if she was really so obsessively concerned with her own appearance, or had she filled her life with these costly trinkets to hide an emptiness she couldn't face?

Her search had turned up no trace of her wedding ring. She went to a small desk by the window and began to open the drawers. There was no sign of the ring, but in the last drawer she found some folded papers. A quick perusal showed these to be a copy of a marriage settlement signed with her name.

She read it in growing astonishment. The settlement transferred her entire holdings in Davison Electronics to Corrado. The value assigned to the shares was staggering, and it was to become his absolutely following the wedding, with, seemingly, no safeguards for herself. What kind of man would propose such a settlement, and how blindly infatuated must she have been to have signed it?

Aunt Claire came into the room, obviously startled at seeing her out of bed. "What are you doing up?"

"I feel much better now," Philippa said, folding the papers away. "I thought I'd get some clues in my belongings, but I don't like what they tell me. I seem to be utterly materialistic and self-centered."

"You're not a bit like that," Aunt Claire said loyally.

"But how well do you know me?"

Claire frowned. "Not well recently," she admitted. "I looked after you for a few years after your mother died, but when you were ten your father brought you to Italy, where he had a factory."

"So that's why I speak Italian?"

"Yes, you were here until you were fifteen. When you returned to England I'd moved to another part of the country, so we haven't seen each other often during the last few years. But you were always a likeable child. Your faults were big, generous ones, and if you hurt people you would always want to do anything in your power to show you were sorry. You could only have grown into a nice person."

Philippa smiled wanly, wishing she could be so certain. "What were you saying just before Corrado came in?" she asked. "It was something about my shocking everyone. What had I done?"

"You broke off your engagement with an Englishman named Michael Radley to marry Corrado. And you'd been engaged to poor Michael for two years."

"Two years?" Philippa echoed in astonishment.

She'd taken two years to decide against Michael Radley and only a few weeks to marry Corrado Bennoni. What kind of spell had he cast to make her plunge recklessly into marriage and strip herself of her possessions? Then she remembered the urgency that had pulsed through her at his touch and heat began to steal over her again. The memory of how he'd laid his hand so tantalizingly close to her breasts brought her body to instant life, so that her nipples peaked and hardened in anticipation of his caresses. This was the answer.

It was only her mind that had forgotten. Her body carried a secret knowledge—part memory, part yearning—deep within her that nothing could erase. It had linked her to Corrado Bennoni, and it would keep her linked to him no matter what the truth about them turned out to be.

"Why don't you come back to England with me?" Claire asked. "I don't want to leave you here with no one to protect you."

"Protect me... from my husband?"

The older woman hesitated. "You do have a very great deal of money, dear," she said delicately.

"And you think Corrado rushed me into marriage to get his hands on it?" Philippa challenged, reluctantly recalling the settlement she'd signed.

"Well...I saw his face when we discovered you'd left, and I didn't like his expression." She jumped as the door opened to reveal Corrado. "I've just been saying that I must go home tomorrow," she said brightly. "And Philippa is going to come with me. She needs a rest, and she'll be better off in her own country..." She faltered under the grave look he was giving her.

"My wife isn't well enough to travel," Corrado said firmly, with a subtle emphasis on "wife." "I'd prefer her to remain where I can supervise her care. Right now she should be in bed." He strode across the room and swept Philippa up into his arms, but instead of carrying her to the bed he stayed where he was, holding her against his muscled chest. Weakness flooded her, making her intensely aware of the power in the arms imprisoning her like steel bands. "Do you want to leave me, Philippa?" he asked quietly.

"No," she said, hearing only the hammering of her heart. "I want to stay."

Two

Aunt Claire returned to England the next day. Philippa remained in bed, cared for by Anna, Corrado's housekeeper, a stout, middle-aged woman with a warm, smiling face. She addressed Philippa as *signora* and treated her as the mistress of the house, but it was clear that she knew the situation because she answered questions without surprise.

Philippa's memory didn't return. She was troubled by a vague feeling that she'd dreamed of Corrado just before she awoke, but she couldn't remember any details, and at last she began to wonder if she'd imagined the whole thing.

The day after her aunt's departure, Corrado came to see her. Like any stranger, he knocked politely on her door and waited until she called. "Why are you up?'' he demanded, noticing her sitting by the window in a blue silk dressing gown, her hair wrapped in a towel.

''It's about time I was,'' she told him firmly. ''I've showered and washed my hair, and now I feel like a new woman.''

He frowned. ''If you wanted to shower you should have called Anna to be with you. You could've fainted.''

''For heaven's sake,'' she said with a laugh, ''I won't break.''

''I'd have thought the evidence showed otherwise,'' he said quietly. She didn't answer, and he walked around the room. He wore a light check shirt, open at the throat so that she could see how the dark, thickly curling hair reached up almost to the base of his neck. He was healthy and glowing, and his movements had an athletic grace that held her eyes.

He stopped in front of Philippa and looked searchingly into her face. ''Has anything come back to you?''

''No, nothing. But I'm sure it will soon. I feel so much better today.''

He leaned down and touched her face, tilting it up toward him. The movement emphasized the lines of her pointed chin, which managed to be delicate and uncompromising at the same time. ''Yes, you do look better. If you're well enough to come downstairs this evening, I'll have dinner served on the terrace.''

''That sounds lovely.''

When he'd gone, Philippa finished drying off her hair, then surveyed her considerable variety of makeup and discovered that she had only the most basic idea of how to use it. The subtleties and nuances of which she'd once, presumably, been mistress had vanished with the rest of her memory. She decided to reproduce the passport picture and at last was pleased with the result.

She selected a scent that was both musky and elusive, hinting at delight promised but deferred. The knowledge of these things lay deep within the body that had quivered with expectancy when he'd touched her earlier. There'd been only thin silk to cover her, and she knew if he'd lowered his eyes he would have detected her response.

The gown she chose for dinner was made of ivory silk and cunningly designed to tempt through concealment. The neck was high but the clinging material outlined the full curves of her breasts, an ambiguity that reflected the situation between herself and the man who was her husband, yet not her husband.

When she'd finished, the invalid with the pale face had been submerged in the glamorous young woman whose green eyes sparkled with anticipation of dinner with a desirable man. The evening to come would be a battle of wits. He wanted to tell her as little as possible, but there were ways of making a man talk when he'd decided not to. She was looking forward to discovering who could outsmart the other.

At ten minutes to eight Corrado came to her door. She had the satisfaction of seeing that her transformation didn't go unnoticed. He stopped dead to take in the glowingly beautiful woman who smiled at him, then recovered and gave her his arm. His own attire was also formal, a dinner jacket and snowy embroidered shirt.

The rest of the house delighted her. It was airy and spacious, with tiled floors, white walls and many arches, a house designed to catch every puff of wind in a hot climate. Corrado led her downstairs and out to a terrace just above ground level. Red, white and pink geraniums decked the stone balustrade, and many more hung in baskets from the roof.

Philippa studied her surroundings with delight. The house was built high on a hill, and from here she could look down over the magnificent bay of Naples, where the lights were already gleaming in the soft air of early summer. "That must be the most beautiful sight in the world," she breathed. She caught his quick glance and added, "Have I said so before?"

"You said something similar when you first saw it a few days ago," Corrado told her. "There was a party to celebrate your arrival. My friends and family all admired you, and you seemed to be enjoying yourself. But then I found you standing on this terrace alone, staring out over the bay."

"It would tempt anyone to stare," she observed, but she hadn't missed the implication that she'd slipped away to brood.

She looked expectantly at Corrado, but instead of pursuing the subject he said smoothly, "Let me show you the grounds while there's still some light."

He led her to a short flight of stone steps descending to the lawn. They followed a path that vanished among bushes and palm trees. Birds called softly to one another in the dusk. Everywhere she saw flowers—red and white oleander, white magnolia, mauve and pink azaleas—all giving their delicate perfume to the evening air. "It's enchanting," she said softly. "But you must have shown it to me before."

"Yes, we walked here together on the evening of your arrival."

What was it like? she wondered. *Did we walk a careful foot apart as we're doing now, or did you slip an arm around my waist and hold me tightly against you?*

"What did I say about it then?"

"Exactly what you said just now, that it's enchanting."

"And what did you reply?"

"That I'd had everything made perfect, in your honor."

But how did you speak? In that polite voice that keeps me at a distance, or softly for my ears alone? Did we keep to these well-regulated paths, or did you pull me into the shadows and kiss me?

The grounds sloped down the hill, and occasionally they came to short flights of steps. Each time Corrado took her arm to steady her and released her as soon as he was sure she was safe. "Let's sit here for a while," he suggested, pointing to a stone seat under the trees that looked out onto the bay.

"I hope you've changed your mind about not telling me about myself," she said.

"No, I still think the best thing is for you to remember of your own accord."

"All right," she said promptly. "Tell me about you, as though I were someone you'd just met."

He hesitated, seeing the snare, and she laughed at his expression. "Look, if we can't talk about me, and we can't talk about you, we shall soon be sitting here in total silence," she said reasonably.

He recovered himself. "Not at all. If I'd just met you I wouldn't waste time talking about myself. I'd tell you how lovely you look."

"It's very kind of you to pay me compliments, Signor Bennoni," she retorted, matching his light tone, "but now I insist that you tell me something about yourself."

"There's very little to tell. I was born in Naples. My family were all fishermen, but I had a mechanical bent so I went to a technical college. I now own a couple of factories that make electrical household goods."

"Was that how you knew my father?"

"We were both concerned with electronics, yes."

He took the glass she was still holding and found a safe place for it. She saw that he was still wearing his wedding band and seized his left hand in both of hers, looking at him questioningly. "We exchanged rings during the civil ceremony," he told her.

"But you've taken mine back, haven't you?"

"I didn't *take* it back," he said with a touch of bitterness. "You left it behind when you ran away. It was you who repudiated our marriage."

"But *why*? Am I..." She colored uncomfortably. "Am I in love with you?"

"Only you can answer that."

"But didn't I ever tell you that I loved you?"

He reached out swiftly and took her by the shoulders. "Philippa, listen to me. You've got to stop asking such questions."

"But I want to know the truth," she cried.

"And will you know it when you hear it?" He moved suddenly, drawing her close, cradling her head against his shoulder and speaking with his lips a few inches from hers. "Yes," he murmured, "you're in love with me. You told me that it was only in my arms that you'd discovered what love meant."

He lowered his mouth until it touched hers with soft, caressing movements. At the feel of his lips on hers her head swam until her own lips fell open, and she waited dizzily for the exploration of his tongue on flesh already grown sensitive in anticipation.

But he didn't deepen the kiss, although the tautness of his muscles told her of his struggle. After a long moment during which she could hear him breathing raggedly, he drew slowly back from her. She wanted to pull his head down again and seek his mouth with her own, demanding the fulfillment of the moment. It hadn't been a kiss. It had been a tantalizing, bewitching, maddening, tormenting half kiss, both a warning and a demonstration of the power he was determined not to abuse.

But every fiber of her being yearned for its completion, no matter what the cost. Frustration at being denied made a small gasp escape from her throat. He heard it and tightened his grip on her shoulders. "Well?" he demanded in a tense voice.

"Well?" she echoed.

"Am I telling the truth, or am I lying to you, knowing that you can't tell the difference? *Did* you say you were in love with me?"

She wanted to cry *yes*, because the thundering of her heart was telling her that it must have been so. But strict honesty forced her to reply bleakly, "I don't know."

"No, and you never will while you have only my word. The scene I've just described never took place. I'm sorry, Philippa, but you had to discover for yourself why I'm doing the wisest thing for both of us."

He released her, and she felt the carousel in her head slow and come to a reluctant halt. But still she couldn't relinquish the bright hope of a moment ago. "Surely, when we spoke of marriage, I must have said something about loving you?" she persisted.

He looked at her. "Not one word," he replied simply.

She expelled a slow breath, feeling as if she'd been punched. Only now did she realize how much it had mattered. She wanted desperately to ask if he loved her, but after what she'd just learned she couldn't get the words out. "I'd like to have my ring back, please," she said after a while.

"I think you should wait until you've had time to decide what you want to do."

"But you're still wearing yours."

"I wasn't the one who rejected our marriage." His voice, already low, became softer still, and through the ominously quiet tone she detected the throb of an anger that had defeated all his efforts to suppress it. "I never made a fool of you, Philippa. I didn't abandon you on our wedding day to the delight and derision of an interested audience. This part of Italy is still very traditional, and the old values still prevail. At one time if a bride had shamed her husband as you did me—" Corrado rose suddenly and strode away from her. Philippa watched him in dismay. He'd seemed so perfectly in command of himself that she'd momentarily forgotten the public insult she'd offered him. But the wound was still raw.

After a moment he returned to her. He was in control of himself again, but she could see the signs of strain, and his voice was taut. "I'm sorry," he said, speaking with an obvious effort. "That was unforgivable of me while you're still not well. You wanted me to tell you about myself, so I'll warn you now that I have a wicked temper. When I'm angry I can say things that tear people apart."

"I'm not a shrinking violet, Corrado," she said, trying to defuse the tension. "What you said didn't hurt me. It barely scratched the surface."

"That's because I stopped myself in time. Sometimes I hardly realize what I'm saying, and I know the dreadful damage I can do. That's why I walked away, because if I'd stayed..." He hesitated as if picking his way among words to select the least dangerous. "You mustn't be hurt, Philippa."

"You have every right to be angry," she conceded, trying to lure him into a revelation.

He shook his head. "There's no such thing as the *right* to wound another person, no matter how much they've injured you, especially when they're vulnerable." Again she had the feeling that he was choosing words with care. "And you are very vulnerable. People are always more defenseless than they seem." He dropped his voice, and she only half caught the last words, "I hope I've learned that much." He drew a painful breath. "Please, Philippa, let's not discuss this yet. I'm not as calm about it as I'd like."

"You can't forgive me, can you?" she asked softly.

As soon as she said "forgive" a mist seemed to clear in her brain, and she saw his face as it had been in the dream, filled with hate and bitterness.

"What is it?" Corrado had seen her suddenly alert expression. "What's happened?"

"Just before I awoke," she said slowly, "I saw you. It was a kind of dream. You were angry with me. I was begging you to forgive me for something, but you said that some wrongs could never be made right. Then I opened my eyes and you were really there. Corrado, you must tell me, what did I do?"

"How can you ask that after what we've just been saying? You humiliated me on our wedding day." His tone assumed a forced lightness. "Not to mention that you wrecked my brand-new car. It would take a very unusual man not to be unreasonable about that."

"No, you're not telling me everything," she said hurriedly. "What is it? *What did I do?*"

He seized her hands, holding them and looking directly into her eyes. "Philippa, I want you to listen to me and accept what I tell you. Apart from the way you deserted me, I have nothing to forgive, and you have nothing to atone for. You don't owe me anything. You've got to believe that."

The strange, intense note in his voice, rather than the words, held her attention. "But how can I?" she asked slowly. "You as much as told me not to believe anything you said."

He drew in his breath sharply. "No, I said your memories must be your own."

"But this *is* my own. I remember you looking at me with hatred."

His grip tightened. "You don't remember it. You dreamed it, and it's left you confused. I can't let you go on thinking things when I know they aren't true. I have no reason to hate you."

His hands were firm and warm, enfolding her own, offering safety in a world where everything was alien. The anger that had flickered in his eyes was gone, leaving only a gentleness that calmed her. She felt the reassurance of his skin against hers and the note of authority in his voice. "Tell me you believe me," he insisted. "Let me hear you say it."

Philippa drew a long, slow breath. "Yes," she said with wonder. "I do believe you...because I trust you. It's strange when I don't know you, but I trust you completely, Corrado."

She could see that her declaration had taken him aback. His face showed his confusion, and a shrewd impulse prompted her to ask, "What's the matter? Didn't I say that last time?"

"Last time?" he parried cautiously.

"Last time I expressed an opinion of your character...whenever that was."

He grinned suddenly. "It was the day we got engaged. You called me an unscrupulous rogue."

"Oh, really? Was that before or after I agreed to marry you?"

"Before."

"You mean, first I called you names, *then* I said yes?" she demanded in astonishment.

"I thought you were very wise. You obviously knew the worst of me, and that's not a bad basis for marriage."

"What *is* the worst of you, Corrado?"

"Among other things, I think the end justifies the means, and sometimes I'm not particular about the means. So beware of thinking too well of me."

"Oh, I didn't say you *weren't* an unscrupulous rogue. I just said I trusted you. It makes perfect sense," she added, enjoying his baffled expression, "to me, anyway. You've told me the truth this time."

"Yes, this is the truth. But how did you know?"

"Because you want to make sure I know the worst of you," she echoed him. "You'll tell me the worst but not the best, because despite what you said, you're an honorable man. I know that about you—" she tapped her breast "—in here, where it matters. What else happened that night?"

But Corrado had recovered from his impulsive burst of frankness, and his defenses were in place again. "It's time we were going in to dinner," he said, drawing her firmly to her feet. "Anna makes an excellent fish soup, and she doesn't like it to be spoiled."

Philippa accompanied him without protest, feeling better than she'd done since she'd awoken in a strange world. The honors of the first round, she thought, were about even.

* * *

As the days slipped by she found that the need to recall her own identity faded beside the need to discover the truth about her relationship with Corrado. It was difficult to believe that she hadn't married him for love when her response to him now was so powerful.

After the kiss in the garden he'd kept a wary distance between them, and she was tormented by the sensations aroused but not fulfilled by that incomplete experience. The touch of his lips on hers had overwhelmed her, and she'd instinctively relaxed, feeling as if her body were beginning to melt in his heat. Then he'd drawn away and forced her to confront the truth, but the real truth was there in his arms, in the clamor of her awakened body.

He'd returned her wedding ring but hadn't offered to put it on her finger himself. At night he slept in a room that adjoined her own, with the connecting door firmly locked. Several times Philippa lay awake listening to his movements on the other side, tensing whenever she heard his footsteps near the door. Once he paused for a long time, and she waited for the sound of his hand on the lock, but the silence stretched on, and at last she heard him moving away. She stared into the darkness, wondering how long she would be forced to live in this limbo—married and yet not married—with no past and a future that she couldn't imagine.

A letter arrived from Aunt Claire enclosing some newspaper cuttings. Those of her father were captioned "Edward Davison, electronics genius," and showed a sturdy, blunt-featured man with a smile that didn't reach his eyes. Aunt Claire had told her she was the center of Edward's world, but to her dismay, Philippa found herself thinking that if she shook hands with the man pictured she would count her fingers afterward.

She had made the gossip pages herself several times, going to opening nights at the theater, dancing till dawn in new nightclubs, always wearing an extravagantly luxurious dress. Before her engagement she seemed to have been a butterfly, whirling about London on the arms of a succession of different men, none of whom lasted very long in her affections. Two years ago she'd become engaged to Michael Radley, and Edward had thrown "the party of the year" according to one gossip columnist. The Ritz ballroom had been the setting, five hundred people had formed the "exclusive" guest list, and enough champagne had been served to float a liner.

The photograph showed her with a stocky young man of medium height with a stubborn chin and a set face. He had his arm fixed possessively around Philippa, as if he'd just won her in a lottery and feared someone else might claim the prize. There was a polite smile on her face, but none of the overflowing joy that could have been expected of a young woman at her engagement party.

She decided that she could easily understand why she'd delayed her marriage to Michael Radley for two years. What baffled her was why she'd gotten engaged to him in the first place.

She was depressed at the view of herself that seemed to have emerged, a decorative socialite with no apparent purpose in life other than to dress expensively and have fun. She said so to Corrado as they stood on the terrace one evening, sipping drinks and watching night fall over the glittering bay. He was wearing an evening shirt, open at the throat in a way that caused her to avert her eyes occasionally. If she looked at him too often she became distracted by how much she wanted to open more buttons and run her fingers through the rough hair of his chest. She was wearing a deceptively simple white dress and had left her hair to flow freely about her shoulders.

"Do you *feel* that's the kind of person you are?" he asked

"No, I can't believe that I've settled for glossy uselessness," she said, frowning. "But how do I know?"

Corrado refilled her glass, and she stood twirling it between her fingers. The glasses were antiques, and the reverent way Corrado had touched them told her a great deal about him. It dawned on her suddenly that the priceless crystal presented an opportunity to discover even more. "How do I know?" she repeated.

"Because if you dislike that kind of person the chances are that you haven't let yourself get that way," he told her. "Trust your instincts, Philippa."

She'd already discovered that she possessed a wry sense of humor with which she could occasionally prick Corrado's gravity. It prompted her to tease him now. "My instincts say that we're causing a public scandal in this part of the world," she murmured.

He looked at her sharply. "Who says so?"

"I was in the village this afternoon. I went to look around the church, and I bumped into the priest. He dropped some heavy hints about setting the date soon. I think he's rather shocked that I'm living here with only a civil ceremony to make me respectable."

"Don Ferrando is a dear old soul, but a little conservative in his views. I'll have a word with him."

"What will you tell him?" she asked lightly. "That you keep the door that connects our rooms locked, so that makes everything all right?"

"If you decide to annul our marriage, it'll be as well that that door is known to be locked."

"Is that your only reason?" she asked slowly.

"What do you mean?"

He had a glass in his hand. Smiling, she held out her own to him. "Would you hold this for a moment?" she asked. He took it in his other hand, giving her a puzzled frown. She stood very close to him, looking up into his face. "I suppose I mean this," she said softly.

She slipped her arm around his neck before he knew what she meant to do. He tensed and made an instinctive movement to push her away. Too late he discovered that his hands were occupied. He had no choice but to stand where he was.

She had leisure now to explore the face whose sensual lines had intrigued her from the first moment. She took her time—caressing his lips, discovering their firm shape, tracing the width with slow movements of her tongue. After his first start of surprise he grew motionless with shock, giving her a chance to slip her other arm around his neck and twine her fingers in his thick, black hair. He felt good to her, as she'd known he would, with an arousing masculine roughness that beguiled, distracted, maddened, provoked and delighted her. She savored him languorously, absorbing the tangy taste of dark maleness spiced with wine, salt and sun.

"Philippa..." he growled warningly when she paused for breath.

She slipped her tongue between his lips before he could close them and felt him tremble. She pressed her body closer to his and arched gently against him while her caressing hands and lips continued their discovery.

Through the roar of her own senses Philippa knew of the fire possessing him and his struggle to subdue it. Now was the time to apply a little more pressure to his overburdened defenses. She began to work on his shirt with nimble fingers. She'd opened two buttons before the sound of breaking glass told her that she'd won. His arms closed around her like a vise, drawing her to him with crushing pressure. He'd taken control and was paying her back in her own coin, kissing her with a passion that equaled hers.

She'd tricked him, forcing him to accept her dangerous gifts. Now he turned the tables on her, taking hungrily and claiming more. His mouth demanded and demanded, yet gave back everything a thousandfold. His movements were skilled, teasing and assaulting her equally. Desire and triumph flooded through her, and she gave herself up to him without reserve.

When they were both breathless he twined his fingers in her hair and pulled her head back so that he could look at her face. She was flushed and gasping slightly, and his hand tightened at the blazing look in her eyes. "You're being very reckless," he said harshly.

"I *am* reckless. When I want something, I want it, and like you, I'm unscrupulous about my methods."

"That's obvious," he said grimly.

She smiled. "Don't be angry with me. I had to know. Now I do."

"And what exactly did you want to know?"

For answer she began to pull him close again, but this time he stopped her. He was breathing deeply, but he had himself in hand. "Oh, no," he growled. "No more risks tonight."

"Why so careful, Corrado?" she taunted, drunk with victory. "What are you afraid of?"

"You," he said simply.

"You want me, don't you?"

"Yes," he said furiously, "I want you, but I've told you how things have to stay between us for the moment."

"Perhaps I have something to say about that."

"Philippa, stop this!" he commanded raggedly. "You're playing with fire."

"I like fire. It's exciting."

"It also burns. I'm going to see that you don't get burned."

"Me? Or yourself?" she challenged.

His only answer was an ironic look, which brought her partly down to earth. Reluctantly she drew herself out of his arms. "I'm sorry about your crystal," she said, surveying the wreckage around their feet.

"To hell with the damned crystal."

She nodded, her eyes dancing. "My sentiments exactly."

He buttoned his shirt right to the top with a gesture of finality. "I think we should go and have dinner."

She took the arm he held out to her. "Are you sure you'll be safe?" she teased.

"Try to control yourself," he admonished her with a reluctant grin. "Remember, the servants will be watching us like hawks after that crash."

She took his arm demurely, and they walked into the house.

She wasn't surprised when the connecting door stayed firmly locked that night. Corrado had recovered and was on his guard. But now they both knew that she'd discovered his vulnerability, and it would be only a matter of time before his resolution collapsed. She promised herself that as she lay watching the closed door.

Three

Philippa returned from a walk one day to find a truck in front of the house. The driver and Anna were staring at each other in a state of mutual incomprehension, and both greeted her with relief. "I've been trying to explain that I have some trunks to deliver," the man told her in English. "They were consigned to this address by a Miss Philippa Davison."

She felt a stab of excitement at the sight of the three large trunks. Surely somewhere in there she would find more clues as to who she was. When they'd all been carried up to her room she shut the door and hunted among her keys for those that fit the locks. Her heart was beating with eagerness and apprehension.

The first trunk was filled with clothes. The second contained books and small ornaments. But in the third she discovered pads of thick white drawing paper in all sizes and a wooden box containing pots of black ink, pens and a large selection of nibs, plus a book entitled *The Technique of Pen and Ink*. She put all this aside for further consideration.

At the very bottom she found papers stacked away in folders. She began to tear them open with shaking fingers, for it was clear she'd come upon the contents of a desk. Here if anywhere she would find her past.

There were letters, some signed by her father, some with names she didn't recognize, but which presumably belonged to friends, but nothing from Corrado. She sighed with disappointment.

She opened the last folder expecting to find another batch of papers, but instead there was a large brown envelope carefully sealed with tape. She ripped it open with a knife and discovered another, similar envelope beneath. The removal of this revealed yet another. Whatever was in this package was something she'd been determined to prevent being seen by the wrong eyes.

At last she reached the final envelope and dumped its contents onto the bed. A mass of photographs flooded out. Feverishly she began to rummage through them, and as she did so the pounding of her heart became deeper and slower.

Almost every picture showed Corrado, but a Corrado she didn't know. He must have been in his early twenties when they were taken, still with the mark of the boy on him, yet showing signs of the man he was to become.

Then she discovered a picture of him in a sailing dinghy with a young girl beside him. Her chestnut hair was tied back in a ponytail, revealing the length of her neck and the finely chiseled lines of her face with its potential beauty. She was gazing at Corrado with blatant adoration.

Philippa stared while her head spun with disbelief and confusion. The girl was herself.

She was many years younger but still recognizable as the root from which the elegant woman of today had grown. She'd thought she'd met Corrado only a month ago, but these pictures told her that she'd known him in her teens.

Why didn't he tell me? she thought wildly.

She hastily turned over the remaining pictures and discovered one of Corrado with his arm around a young woman, attractive in a slightly hard way, who'd positioned her left hand to display an engagement ring. By chance the photographer had also caught Philippa in the background, frowning at Corrado's fiancée.

She sat staring at what she'd discovered, aware that long vistas had opened up, not in front as they usually did, but behind her. Her knowledge of Corrado stretched back for many years. If she'd read her own face accurately she'd had a youthful infatuation for him, yet a few weeks ago she'd agreed to their marriage without one word of love.

She began to read the letters. There were only two from her father. These seemed to have been written while he was on vacation and were brief and factual. He was obviously fond of her but wrote like a businessman, despite the fact that she was his daughter.

The letter that held her attention was from The Burford Gallery in London, thanking her for her latest consignment of pen-and-ink drawings and assuring her that these would sell as well as her other work. Philippa drew a breath of pleasure and relief. At last she could discard the vision of herself as nothing but a rich man's socialite daughter. Probably her work didn't earn very much, but at least she'd done something.

The letter ended:

> I was relieved to learn from you that your forthcoming marriage won't interfere with your work. The area around Naples should provide you with many subjects of the kind in which you specialize.

It was signed, Edwin R. Hungerford, Director.

But what kind of subject do I specialize in? Philippa wondered.

That night she took out the photographs and laid them before Corrado in silence. Watching his face she detected the slight tightening that revealed his displeasure. "It's you and me, isn't it?" she asked. "Years ago."

"Yes," he said.

"We knew each other when I lived in Naples. You should have told me that."

"You know why I don't tell you about the past. We've been over this."

"But you let me think we'd only known each other a month."

"In a sense we have. You were fifteen when these were taken, and after you returned to England we didn't see each other for eight years. What happened long ago is irrelevant."

"If it's irrelevant it wouldn't have done any harm to tell me," she pointed out, and saw that her shrewdness had disconcerted him. "I don't think it *is* irrelevant, and I want to know what happened. How well did we know each other?"

He shrugged. "I worked for your father. You were always running in and out of the factory, and his employees regarded you as a kind of mascot. We were all fond of you."

"But I attached myself to you, didn't I? You took me to meet your family. This *is* your family?" She indicated a picture of him with a middle-aged man and woman and a young man whose face had a slight similarity to his own.

"Yes. You insisted on meeting them because you wanted to come out in the boat. You've always loved the sea."

"Is this man your brother?"

"No, my cousin Paolo. I have no brothers or sisters, but my mother always wanted a girl, and she practically adopted you. You came and went in our house as though it was your own." He shuffled the pictures until he came to the one of the two of them in a boat. "That little blue dinghy is called *The Swallow*. I used it for teaching you to sail. My father's dead now, and my mother's gone to live in Pozzuoli, farther down the coast, where she has a widowed sister."

It was rare for Corrado to add details like this, and something told Philippa he was doing it to put off the moment when she'd ask him about the picture of himself with the young woman. She pulled it forward determinedly. "You were engaged to her, weren't you?" she asked.

"Yes."

"Did you ever marry? Are you a widower?"

After a moment he answered, "We never married."

"Why?" she persisted.

There was constraint in Corrado's voice as he replied, "Her father wanted a rich man for his daughter. I promised him I'd make my fortune. When I failed he urged her to break the engagement and marry someone else. She did."

"Is she still in Naples?"

"No, her husband is a banker in Milan. What else did you discover today?"

Plainly he was determined not to talk about his ex-fiancée. Philippa longed to ask if the past still hurt him, but his face was as smooth and unrevealing as his voice, and she knew this wasn't the right moment. She began to tell him about her drawings. "It's nice to know I'm good at something," she said. "All I have to do now is discover what I specialize in."

"Can I see the letter?" Corrado asked pleasantly.

Philippa produced it, and he studied the words with a frown on his face. "Tantalizing," he agreed.

"Did you ever see any of my drawings?"

"Yes, but only briefly. I can't give you a clear idea of them, except that they were mostly buildings. You had a liking for ruins with plenty of atmosphere."

"In any case, I need to see them for myself," she said, smothering a sleepy yawn. The conflicting emotions of the day had left her worn-out. "I think I should go to London and look at the drawings I recently sent this gallery. Who knows what else I might remember?"

Corrado nodded. "That's an excellent idea."

"Then why don't I go at once? I'm tired of sitting here waiting for something to happen."

"That's natural," he said, smiling at her determined expression. "But could you delay your trip a little? I'm having an important business contact to dinner in a few days. He's bringing his fiancée, so it would look better if my wife was with us."

"I could just look at the pictures and come back quickly," she objected. She was reluctant to postpone the prospect of a discovery.

"But you probably won't want to. You'll have a great deal to do, old friends to look up, and it would be a nuisance to have to return early."

She sighed. "You're right, I suppose. All right, I'll wait."

"Thank you." He took a close look at her. "You're tired. You've had too much excitement for one day."

"I'm fine," she protested, laughing. "You mustn't treat me like a sickly child."

Corrado shrugged. "It's natural for a man to take care of his wife."

It was the first time he'd referred to her as his wife in that unthinking way, and he reddened as soon as the words were out of his mouth. "Don't stay up too late," he said briefly.

"I'll go to bed now," she agreed, but remained where she was, unwilling to face the task of rising. "I think you'll have to help me," she said, reaching out her hands to him.

He pulled her to her feet and steadied her against him. For a moment she felt the warmth of his breath on her cheek and sensed the temptation that racked him. Then he kissed her on the forehead. "Good night... wife," he murmured.

"Good night," she whispered, dazed with longing and frustration.

She made her way sleepily up the stairs. As she reached the top she heard the phone ring. It was answered at once, as though Corrado had quickly grabbed the receiver. She thought she heard him angrily say, "I'm sorry, you have the wrong number," followed by the sound of the receiver being slammed down. It was only later, when she was almost asleep, that it occurred to her that he'd been speaking English.

On the day Giorgio Rossi and his fiancée were due for dinner, Philippa went into the kitchen to find Anna loudly complaining that the wine merchant had failed to deliver her order. To calm her, Philippa offered to drive to the village.

She collected the wine without trouble, but after that nothing seemed to go right. Her car wouldn't start, the village's one taxi was already taken, and when she tried to call home to explain her predicament she couldn't get through.

In exasperation at the late hour, she called information. "That number has been changed," the operator told her.

"Can you give me the new number, please?"

"I'm sorry, *signora*, the new number is not in the directory."

"*What?* It must be! It's my home."

"I'm afraid I'm not allowed to give it out."

Nothing Philippa said would persuade the operator. The taxi collected her an hour later, and she hastened home to find Corrado waiting anxiously on the step. A glance at his pale face told her that he was reliving her previous disappearance. "Don't ever worry me like that again," he snapped as they went upstairs.

"Don't blame me," she told him indignantly. "How could I let you know what had happened when you'd changed the number without telling me?"

Corrado made a sound of annoyance with himself. "I'm sorry. I forgot."

She paused at her bedroom door to demand, "What was wrong with the old number?"

"Too many wrong numbers. Hurry up and get ready. They'll be here any minute."

"But why an unlisted number?"

"Same reason. Philippa, will you *please* get ready?"

"But—"

She found herself being propelled into her room, and the door shut firmly behind her. "Get ready!" Corrado yelled from the other side.

She managed to be on the front step beside him in half an hour and saw his eyebrows lift. "You performed a miracle," he said, surveying the softly draped jade dress and gold accessories with admiration.

"Will I be able to hold up my head in front of Giorgio Rossi's fiancée?" she asked lightly.

"You needn't fear comparisons with any other woman, but I know nothing about this lady. They've only just gotten engaged."

"How much does Giorgio know about me?"

"Only that you're my wife. He lives in Milan. He won't know about your amnesia or what happened on our wedding day. He isn't a friend, although we're on good terms, just a business associate."

A car appeared around the bend in the road and in a moment had drawn up before them. The occupants revealed themselves as a large man in his forties and a voluptuous, dark-haired woman. They advanced to greet their hosts, and the welcoming smile froze on Philippa's face.

She was looking at Maria, the woman Corrado had once loved.

Four

Maria gave Corrado a brilliant smile of recognition and held out her hand to him. As if in a dream he took it. "Maria..." Philippa could hear the shock in his voice.

Maria chuckled deeply. "I told Giorgio that you and I knew each other years ago and made him promise not to tell you I was coming. Surprised?"

"Yes," he said slowly. He seemed to pull himself together with an effort. "But of course I'm delighted to see you again. This is my wife."

Philippa shook hands mechanically while she studied the other woman and realized that she was being studied in return. The slight hardness that had once been in Maria's face was more pronounced now, and her expression, even when smiling, was carefully controlled. She was expensively dressed in white, a color far too young for her ripe looks, and she blazed with jewelry. Her perfume was heavy and musky, the scent of a woman determined not to be overlooked.

Philippa heard herself uttering conventional words of welcome, and then Corrado was leading them all into the house. She began to dispense drinks, uttering meaningless platitudes to Giorgio and trying to resist the temptation to eavesdrop on the other two. She just caught Corrado's words, "...no idea your husband had died," before she forced herself to turn away.

But Corrado's face remained imprinted on her mind as it had looked when he first saw Maria. He'd been astounded at meeting this ghost from the past, his poise fractured as Philippa had never seen it before. She remembered how edgy he'd become at the mention of Maria's name, as if it still brought back too much pain to bear. And now he'd found that his one-time love was free, while he himself was in the coils of a half marriage.

The conversation became general. Maria was talking about her husband, the Milanese banker. "He died a year ago," she said huskily, "and of course I've lived very much alone. But dear Giorgio said I should get out more, and since then we've gotten closer every day."

"That's delightful," Corrado said with a smile. "I congratulate you both." He sounded tortured through the formal words.

Anna called them to dinner, and they went out to the terrace where the table was laid. Maria demanded Corrado's attention, leaving Philippa to talk to Giorgio, who seemed a pleasant, straightforward man.

"I've known Corrado for years," he told her. "I manufacture some of the components he uses—plugs, valves, cable, et cetera." He grinned. "Of course we try to bargain each other down constantly."

"Who usually wins?" Philippa asked.

"He's *always* won, ever since we signed our first contract, seven years ago. He was in his twenties. He'd come from nowhere and persuaded a bank to lend him enough money to buy a factory that was going bankrupt. I thought I was dealing with a real Johnny Raw. That was my mistake. He not only got me to drop the price but persuaded me to have a valve redesigned because *he* said it wasn't good enough. He was right, too.

"It's been like that ever since. He learned the business end of things by trial and error, but he already knew more about electronics than any other ten men I've met. But I must be telling you what you already know."

"Only in outline," Philippa said cautiously. "Corrado hasn't told me details about his early days as a manufacturer, and I'm interested. Please go on."

"Well, since then he's grown quite a bit. He's still a very small trader by world standards, but he's a lot bigger than when he started. He's expanded into a second factory—one I had my eye on actually—but he got there first. Now he wants to take over mine and manufacture my components under license."

"Are you going to let him?"

"I don't have a lot of choice. If I refuse, he's likely to design his own components. He's such a design wizard that he could easily put me out of business." Giorgio laughed comfortably. "As a matter of fact this is a very good deal for me. Corrado is one of the most honorable men I know. It's just that he will insist on everyone doing things his way."

"Yes," Philippa mused wryly, "I know what you mean."

"Maria says he's always been like that," Giorgio continued. "She comes from these parts and used to know his family."

"So I believe," Philippa said noncommittally. "It must be pleasant for her to look up old friends."

"Yes, she was very eager to come with me. Not that we'll get to see anyone else. We haven't much time."

His relaxed tone made it clear that he didn't know of his fiancée's youthful engagement and was completely unsuspicious about this meeting. But Philippa's suspicions were flashing a red alert.

As they rose from the table, Corrado contrived to draw her aside and murmur, "You've obviously recognized Maria. I'm sorry, Philippa, I didn't know who Giorgio's fiancée was. I wouldn't have knowingly put you in this position. You can slip off to bed in five minutes. I've already said you have a headache."

"Oh *have* you?" she exclaimed, incensed. "Well, you can just tell them I've made a miracle recovery. I'm not running away. I'm going to stay right here and fight it out." She met his eye. "Who knows? I might find Maria a very interesting companion."

His mouth tightened in annoyance, but he was forced to turn away as Maria laid a hand on his arm. "You have such a beautiful garden," she said. "Why doesn't Philippa show me around while you and Giorgio get on with your talk?"

"Certainly," Philippa said at once.

"I wouldn't dream of neglecting my guests like that," Corrado intervened quickly. "I'll take you myself."

"I'm going to stay here and enjoy talking to my hostess," Giorgio announced. Oblivious to the charged atmosphere, he settled himself comfortably in a chair by the drinks table and poured himself another brandy.

Philippa tried to make good use of the ensuing half hour, but Giorgio knew little beyond what he'd already told her. It was Maria she needed to talk to, and Corrado had blocked that . . . unless he'd had another reason for wanting to escort her himself. Philippa's imagination followed them through the moonlit gardens while she vainly assured herself she was indulging foolish fancies.

At last she heard the sound of voices coming from the darkness between the trees. As Corrado and Maria emerged she tried not to look at them too obviously, ashamed of the jealousy that tore at her. But she couldn't help seeing how Maria had her arm through his, or the way she tightened it suddenly so that she squeezed her curvaceous body against him as she laughed up into his face. Corrado smiled back, but the angle of his head made it impossible for Philippa to see his eyes and discover his true feelings.

As the other two reached the terrace, Giorgio produced some papers and said heartily, "Well, I suppose we should do some work."

Maria beamed at Philippa. "Let's leave the men to their boring talk. I do so want to get to know you."

Before Philippa could answer, Corrado said, "But my wife doesn't find business boring, and I want her to be part of all my decisions." His tone was pleasant but underlined with steel, and he guided Philippa firmly to a chair close to his own.

"In general, yes," she responded, trying to be equally firm, "but since we have guests I'll waive the privilege for tonight."

She tried to move to another chair, but Corrado had his arm around her shoulders in what looked like a gesture of affection. Only the two concerned knew that he was keeping her there by exerting his superior strength. "It's not a privilege, *cara*," he said, smiling at her. "Since you're a member of the board it's a necessity."

"Since when did I become a member of the board?" she murmured, attempting to ease away from his arm.

"As of this moment," he murmured back, not budging.

Their eyes met. His were smiling but determined. "You are utterly unscrupulous," she said in an explosive undertone.

He grinned. "You said that before."

"Well, since I don't remember that, I'll give myself the pleasure of saying it again. Of all the disgraceful, cheating—"

"Oh, no!" The smile in his eyes changed to a glint. "I don't cheat. I stick to the rules."

"But who makes these rules?" she demanded indignantly.

"I do, naturally."

"All right, I give in, *for the moment*. I'll have to develop some more cunning before I take you on."

He tightened his arm, leaning down until his mouth was close to hers. "Don't try it, *cara*," he whispered. "I learned my methods in a harder school than you could ever dream of."

He closed her mouth with his own before she could answer, and she felt his warm breath caressing her seductively. Sensations chased through her, but almost at once Corrado drew back. Philippa became aware of the other two watching them, Giorgio with a grin and Maria with a cold stare. "Don't mind us," Giorgio chuckled. "We'll be newlyweds ourselves soon, won't we, darling?"

Maria's only response was a mechanical smile. Her eyes were still on Philippa, and the hardness about her mouth was very pronounced.

The serious talk began. The two men were negotiating the contract that would give Corrado control of Giorgio's local factory, and Philippa found that she understood a good deal about the subject. Once Giorgio made a neat pun on a piece of engineering jargon, and she laughed. Maria sighed. "I'm afraid that went over my head," she complained.

Philippa turned slightly away from the table and explained the play on words. "And you really understand when they say things like that?" Maria asked. "My goodness, how clever you must be."

"It's not cleverness, it's just that..." Philippa paused uneasily, realizing that she didn't know the explanation. "It's in my blood," she finished.

"Of course, you were practically brought up in the factory, weren't you?" Maria murmured. "Not to mention the way you insisted on living in Corrado's pocket."

Philippa's heart began to beat faster, but she shrugged as she said, "That's rather an exaggeration, surely?"

Maria gave a soft, silvery laugh. "My dear, if anything, it's an understatement. You were always hanging around him. Poor Corrado didn't know how to get rid of you. Of course, if you'd been any other girl he'd have told you to stop embarrassing him, but you were the boss's daughter."

A chill spread over Philippa's heart, but she forced herself to speak casually. "Are you saying he discussed me with you?"

The sensual, reminiscent smile on the other woman's face made Philippa clench her hands. "Ricky and I were passionately in love," Maria said softly.

"Ricky?"

"That's what I called him. He liked it because no one else ever called him that, and of course Riccardo is his second name." Maria sighed. "I do hope you don't use it."

"No," Philippa said with difficulty. Maria's smile showed that she'd guessed Philippa didn't even know her husband's second name.

"Ricky told me everything," she went on. "He called you 'the gawky pest,' which was rather unkind, but I'm afraid he has a streak of cruelty." Maria gave a little shudder of delight. "That's what makes him such an exciting lover . . . isn't it?"

Her eyes held Philippa's. They were hard and challenging, as if this woman who'd known Corrado intimately were taunting the wife who'd never been allowed to share his bed. Their voices hadn't risen above murmurs, but the air was alive with their hostility. "And yet you married someone else," Philippa mused with a faint satirical smile that revealed no hint of the pain she was enduring.

Maria gave an elegant shrug. "What else could I do? Corrado wanted to shower me with diamonds. When he realized it was a hopeless dream he insisted on ending our engagement. He was so proud. But we both knew we'd never forget—" Maria checked herself and smiled with acid sweetness. "I must admit that you had the last laugh, though," she murmured. "I couldn't compete with the Davison millions."

Philippa took a long breath to steady herself. She wanted to shout that it wasn't true, that Corrado couldn't have married her for her wealth, but what did she know of him? Still, she wasn't going to let Maria get away with that, unchallenged. "You would naturally see it in those terms," she said in a low, icy voice. "I imagine money's the only thing you understand."

Maria's composure fractured just a little. "I don't think it's for Edward Davison's daughter to lecture me about money—" she began.

"Philippa!" Corrado's voice cut across them.

She pulled herself together. "I'm sorry. I let my attention wander."

"I wish you'd concentrate. This is important." His eyes moved sharply between the two women.

Philippa turned back to the table and forced herself to take an interest in the negotiations. She soon grasped that Corrado was an astute businessman with a razor-sharp appreciation of the other man's potential weaknesses and a determined refusal to take advantage of them. It was clear, too, that he intended to finance the deal through a local bank without making any use of Philippa's money. "Look here," he said, thrusting the draft contract at Giorgio and indicating a long paragraph. "Have you taken in all the implications?"

Giorgio grinned. He'd been growing progressively more genial as the level of brandy grew lower in the decanter. "Probably not," he said easily. "Life's too short to be suspicious. I know you won't cheat me."

"Thank you, but I think you ought to be," Corrado said firmly. "There's a loophole here that you should be aware of."

Philippa listened to him rewording the paragraph and wondered how many businessmen were so conscientious to their own disadvantage. He was an honorable man, she told herself determinedly. That was why he wouldn't let her commit herself to him while she was confused. Maria's insinuations were prompted by jealous spite. She *must* believe that.

At last it was all over, and the men were shaking hands. Corrado put out his hand to Maria, but she ignored it and kissed him, saying, "It's so wonderful to see you again, *dearest Ricky*. What friends we're all going to be."

By then even the easygoing Giorgio had gotten the message. He took firm hold of Maria and didn't let go until they were in the car. Philippa smiled and waved politely, avoiding Corrado's eyes, although she knew he was watching her. "What a small world," she said with forced cheerfulness.

"I know you're angry, and you have every right to be," Corrado began.

"I'm not angry," she assured him as they went inside the house. But in fact she was angry enough to enjoy knowing that his nerves were as stretched as her own, and he was awaiting her reaction warily. "I'm looking forward to a long friendship with Maria."

The words were tinged with irony, and Corrado flushed. "You won't have to see her again, I'll make sure of that," he said quickly. "Obviously she said something that offended you. You'd better tell me what it was."

"She didn't say anything that I need to go running to you about," Philippa told him firmly.

She saw his face darken with annoyance at being thwarted. "I'd still like to know," he persisted.

"I'm sure you would." She faced him. "Why don't you just tell me what you're *afraid* she said? Then I'll tell you whether she did."

Corrado looked at her with appreciation. "It seems that neither of us is going to yield," he said. "So let's drop this unprofitable subject."

"Then I'm going to bed. I want a good night's sleep if I'm traveling tomorrow."

"Traveling?"

"You haven't forgotten that I'm going to England?"

"No, but—come here a moment." He took her hand and led her into the large room that opened onto the terrace. "I have a gift for you. It only arrived today." He opened a cupboard, took out a large, heavy parcel and placed it on the table. "Open it," he said.

Puzzled, Philippa began to open the cardboard. When she had the contents laid out on the table she surveyed them with wonder. There were ten framed pen-and-ink drawings. Most of them were of buildings, castles and ruins, all with a mysterious, magical atmosphere. Whoever had created them had a vivid imagination and the expertise to bring dreams to life. Philippa touched them reverently and holding her breath ran her eyes over the signatures. Every picture was signed P. Davison.

"They're your own work," Corrado told her. "I bought everything the gallery had."

Thoughts chased one another madly across Philippa's brain. There was a moment's delight at the discovery of her own skill, but it was quickly swamped in the rage that welled up in her. "Corrado, how dare you do this!"

He didn't answer, and she turned sharply away and began to stride up and down the room. She was shaking with the force of her own fury, knowing that behind it lay a nameless fear. "You had no right," she choked.

"You're angry because I bought you a gift?" he asked quietly.

"It's not a gift," she exploded. "It's a way of controlling me. You didn't do it to help me, you did it to stop me from going to England. Now I know why you asked me to wait a few days. And if the drawings hadn't arrived this morning, I guess there'd have been another excuse for delay. What game are you playing, Corrado?"

"I'm not playing games," he said, very pale. "This is too serious."

"What is it that's so serious I mustn't be allowed to find out?" she flung at him.

"Philippa, please believe me, I don't want to stop you learning the truth. I only want you to remember it in the right way."

"*Your* way! Controlled and managed by you. That's not good enough. I don't only want your truth, I want the whole truth, and I'm going to have it. I'm tired of being manipulated while you decide what it's right for me to know. *I'll* decide that. I want you to tell me everything, at once. No more evasions."

"But don't you understand that I can't tell you 'everything'? I don't know everything, only a few facts, which are dangerously incomplete. I can't tell you the important things, like what you thought or felt on our wedding day. You've got to remember those things for yourself."

"How can I if you won't help me? I'm going to England, Corrado. I'll find people there who'll tell me what I want to know."

"You'll find people who'll tell you what suits them," he said harshly.

"And isn't that what you're doing?" she cried. After the strain of the last few weeks something had snapped in her mind. "I can't endure living in a vacuum any longer. I want to know who I am *inside*. I want to know what there's been between us and what you feel for me . . . if anything."

"If anything?" he asked with suppressed violence, pulling her into his arms.

But instead of melting at his touch as she'd done in the past, Philippa was angry enough to twist away from him. For the moment her passion for Corrado was less important than her need for the truth. Corrado felt her trying to free herself and held her firmly. He was used to Philippa using her allure to try to weaken his resolve. Now, as he saw the defiance in her eyes, he realized that she was no longer asking but demanding. He'd incautiously let her see how much he dreaded her return to England and thereby given her a weapon with which she could change the terms of their battle. From now on she'd pick the ground and dictate the strategy, forcing him onto the defensive.

But though his mind knew this, his instincts made him refuse to admit defeat. He didn't release her but used all his strength to draw her closer, knowing he was acting dangerously. As she writhed against his body, the shock from that contact spread out and enveloped him.

He kissed her with angry desperation, as though he were battling with himself while his lips plundered hers, reminding her silently of what they were beginning to share—something so sweet that all other questions seemed meaningless. Philippa felt herself yielding against her will to that hypnotic spell. The flame of her fury was being transmuted into another kind of fire, and at last she gave up struggling and strained eagerly against him. It was so easy to forget everything but her passion when she was in his arms. The words that had signified so much a moment ago retreated into a distant hum, leaving the desire that Corrado had ignited.

His caresses grew more urgent as he sensed the responsive heat of her body, communicating itself to him until his very bones seemed to melt. Her lips held witchery, casting a spell of black magic that swept away his stern resolutions like twigs in a forest fire. "If anything," he repeated softly, looking down at her hazy eyes and tousled hair. "Does this tell you what you want to know?"

"No," she murmured, aching with longing. "I won't know until we make love."

"The truth can't always be found with the body," he said huskily. "Only another kind of illusion."

"Not for us. Take me now, Corrado."

Fevered images of everything he wanted to do with her chased through his brain. He tried to blot them out, but they persisted, becoming more entrancing. He wanted her in every way—in his arms, in his bed, beneath him, enfolding him, seducing him with mouth and loins, until he could forget everything else in the world and utterly lose himself in her.

Philippa saw the struggle reflected in his face, and for a moment she thought she'd won. She reached up to kiss him again, but he jerked sharply away, his voice shaking. "Don't make things difficult for us both," he pleaded. "Trust me."

Bitter disappointment made her cruel. "Why should I? I don't know you," she said with a flash of anger. "How many times have you told me that my amnesia means I don't know who to trust? Well, now I come to think of it, you're perfectly right, and that includes you."

She saw his mouth tighten at the neat way she'd turned his own arguments back against him. "Let's face it," she went on, not taking her eyes from him any more than she would have done a tiger, "none of the things I've learned about you are encouraging, are they? I married you, but I seem to have changed my mind pretty quickly. Why don't you tell me why?"

"Because I don't know why!" he shouted.

"Neither do I." She laughed brittlely. "Who knows what I might have discovered? Maybe you have a wife and six children somewhere."

"Don't be ridiculous!"

"Who's to say it's ridiculous? You? Why should I believe you? I know you're hiding things from me. I want the truth, Corrado, and I don't care what I have to do to get it."

"My God, you *are* Edward Davison's daughter, aren't you?" he said with sudden bitterness.

"That's the second time tonight someone's seen me in terms of my father," she said. "Maria said it wasn't for Edward Davison's daughter to lecture her about money. What did she mean?"

Corrado's face was pale. "Probably that your father was famous in this region as a tightfisted skinflint. He exploited his workers and paid them the lowest wages he could get away with. That's why he came to Italy. The labor was cheaper. He was also cynical and unscrupulous. Perhaps you're a chip off the old block."

"If I am, it makes us birds of a feather," she said with a laugh. "Didn't I say something like that about you?"

"Yes, but I'm an amateur compared to the Davisons, father and daughter." A strange look came over Corrado's face, and Philippa had an unnerving feeling that he was seeing past her. "The same ruthlessness, the same ability to pinpoint a man's weak spot and go for it—"

"Corrado." She shook him lightly. He stared as though a mist had suddenly cleared and revealed her. "Corrado," she repeated, "are you trying to tell me that you hate me?"

"No, I don't hate you. It's not as simple as that. The situation between us is . . . complicated. I'm only asking you to be patient. Please wait a little longer."

"I've waited long enough. Now I'm going to do things my way. I'm going back to England tomorrow."

"No."

"Don't try to stop me."

"In England you'll find nothing but distortions. The truth is here."

"Then help me find it," she cried passionately.

"And if I do, will you promise me—"

"The only promise I'll make is that if you don't help me, I'll go and find those who will."

"In other words," he said grimly, "this isn't a bargain. It's a threat."

"Yes. As you said, I'm Edward Davison's daughter. I gather that's what he would've done, and he seems to have gotten results."

Corrado's mouth twisted bitterly. "Oh, he got results all right. Very well. Tomorrow we'll go back to the place where you lived as a child. It's empty now. You can go over it and see what happens. I always meant to take you there when you were a little stronger. But I guess you picked your own time."

Five

Philippa was downstairs early the next morning, half expecting Corrado to have some excuse for delaying their expedition and ready to do battle if he did. There was no sign of him, but after a moment she heard him talking on the telephone in the room he used as an office. He was speaking English, and he sounded commanding. "That's quite enough," he snapped. "I'm not impressed with your excuses. I made it clear in my letter that copies of all reports were to be sent to me, and I meant *all* reports."

He paused. Philippa had gone to stand in the doorway, from where she could just make out that someone on the other end of the receiver was also angry. Corrado interrupted, "That may have been good enough in the old days, but those days are gone. You'll all learn that soon enough when I get over there and start making changes."

Another pause, then Corrado spoke more harshly than Philippa could ever remember. "You may be the managing director but fifty-one percent of Davison Electronics now belongs to me, and the sooner you learn to do things my way the better it'll be for everyone concerned." He put down the receiver abruptly and looked up to see her watching him.

"So we *all* have to do things your way, don't we?" she said wryly. She'd been disturbed by the way Corrado had flattened opposition like a man crushing twigs beneath his boots. There'd been no attempt at conciliation, no suggestion that there might be another point of view, just a blunt assertion of power. Yet this was the same man who refused to use his own power over her. If she could only find the key to the mingling of his dark and light sides, she might begin to understand his hold on her heart, a painful hold that grew stronger by the day.

He shrugged. "I happen to believe that my way is right. You put your inheritance into my hands. One day you may decide to take it back, but until you do I must run it as I think best."

"And that includes driving over the managing director like an armored tank?"

"He's a disaster. If I could have gotten over there sooner, he'd have been replaced already." He saw her frowning and added quietly, "Would you like to take over?"

"How can I?" she asked helplessly. "I don't know anything about running a big company. Or do I?"

"No. You know a good deal about the firm, but you couldn't run it."

"You spoke of going to England and making changes," Philippa said with a glimmer of inspiration.

"Yes, I must."

"Obviously, if they're not sending you all the necessary paperwork. You've got problems at this distance."

Corrado's eyes gleamed. "What are you getting at, Philippa?"

"I think we should both go to England now and sort things out."

He grinned. "One day we will, but today we have an appointment to see your old home. Don't tell me you've forgotten that?" He slipped an arm around her shoulders before she could reply. "Let's have some breakfast and be off. You're looking very lovely this morning."

She'd tried to look beautiful for him and had dressed with great care in beige linen slacks and a green silk shirt, set off by gold earrings. His remark, plus the warmth in his gaze, disconcerted her. He added to her agitation by brushing his lips against hers, allowing them to linger just long enough to addle her wits, and by the time she was clearheaded again they were seated at the table, and she was facing the fact that Corrado had won another round.

She drank her coffee hurriedly, too nervous to eat. When they started the journey she realized that he, too, was on edge. He drove fast down the steeply sloping roads, and gradually the view of Naples vanished until all she could see were the twin craters of Vesuvius looming through the distant mist.

They were in open country, speeding along roads lined with ditches that marked the boundaries of vineyards and fields filled with corn. Now and then they passed houses with red tile roofs and stucco walls. Gradually the houses grew closer together, until she realized that they must have reached the outskirts of Naples. Corrado turned the car down a dusty track. "Nearly there," he said.

Philippa examined her surroundings eagerly, trying to find anything that looked familiar, but everything was strange. Corrado slowed the car as the path became more overgrown. "Here we are," he declared.

They'd reached a small villa that stood on its own modest grounds. House and land presented an appearance of long neglect, with weeds growing almost waist-high around a shuttered building that turned blind eyes to them. Despite the warm day Philippa shivered slightly. There was something unwelcoming about this place.

They walked around the back, seeking an entrance, and at last discovered a door where the wood was so rotten that it needed only a push to open it. A musty staleness assailed Philippa's nostrils as she went inside and ducked a cobweb. Corrado flung open the shutters, flooding the room with light, revealing that the house was almost empty.

He began to lead her through the rooms. "This was the kitchen, where I once showed you how to cook fish."

"You?"

He grinned. "Every Italian man is a good cook, and every Neapolitan is an expert on fish. I was here one day when you were practicing a dish you'd learned from Tina, your father's housekeeper. I told you it was all wrong and showed you how to do it properly, and Tina came in while we were talking. She and I argued vehemently, and she chased me out with a frying pan."

She laughed as he'd meant her to and found that her tension had eased. She tried to picture the scene, the Italian housewife, indignant at being challenged in her own kitchen, the young man laughing at her, arrogantly sure that the right way would always be *his*. And herself, siding with him because she adored him. It was sad to have lost something that must have been so funny and delightful.

"This was your father's study," he said, leading her into a large room at the back of the house. "His desk was there by the window, and that wall next to it was filled with books. You were always in and out of this room. Your father loved having you around."

She thought of the heavyset man that she'd seen in the newspaper picture. Here he'd sat, perhaps working out some of the projects that had made him a giant in his field. But when she'd come into the room the work would have been laid aside, and those crafty eyes would have softened into warmth. Had she smiled back, returning love for love?

Corrado led her back into the hall. "The upstairs room on the corner used to be yours. I know because you once called to me out of the window."

She hurried up to her old bedroom. It was small and poorly lit. She threw open the shutters and leaned out to see Corrado in the garden below. "Like this?" she called.

"That's right."

She looked at him standing below, the sun on his dark skin, his whole body radiating vitality. Her imagination tried to conjure up Corrado as he must have been on that far-off day, eager, laughing, full of confidence. He was gone now, and in his place lived a man who was full of a sad tension that never quite left him even when he smiled. Philippa shook herself, trying to dismiss the youthful ghost she'd invoked, but he wouldn't go. He stood there, silently warning her that someday she must confront him.

She saw Corrado turn back into the house and hurried down the stairs to meet him. "Shall we go now?" he asked.

"But surely I haven't seen the whole house," she objected. "What about that door just behind you?"

He hesitated, then pushed open the door, revealing a narrow, empty room that looked out onto the garden. Philippa went in and looked around her, noting the large windows that let in streaming sunlight. "It would be an ideal place for an artist," she said instinctively.

"Yes, I believe you used to do some drawing in here," Corrado said with a shrug.

"That's right, I did," she agreed eagerly. "I made this my hobby room because my bedroom was too small."

"You remember that? What else?" he demanded, taking a swift, urgent step toward her.

"Nothing. I just knew suddenly that I'd spent a lot of time here." Philippa began to move frantically about the room, trying to force her memory into life. Images came and went in her mind, always vanishing too swiftly for her to catch them. She had a tormenting certainty that the truth lay only just out of reach. She was closer now than she'd ever been before, with only an invisible veil barring her way.

"I spent a lot of time here," she repeated. "And I—and once—" The words were choked off as a sense of dread pressed in on her. She was being suffocated, but she fought to seize the memories while there was time. "Once—" she gasped again. She was trembling, and tears poured down her face.

"Philippa." Corrado stood beside her and called her compellingly. He took hold of her shoulders and shook her to get her attention. "Philippa!"

"No." She tried to push him away. "I must try to—" But the anguish was too much. It swamped her mind, making her shudder, and she let him pull her into his arms. He held her close while she wept with uncontrollable grief for the past and its hidden tragedies, and with despair for the chance she'd lost.

"It's all right," he murmured, gently stroking her hair. "I'm here. Hush."

"I nearly remembered," she whispered. "But I drew back because I was afraid. What am I running away from? Was I so awful that I have to hide from myself?"

To her relief he laughed with genuine amusement. "Now you're being absurd. I knew you when you were fifteen, and you were a normal, happy young girl. You weren't awful, *cara*, I promise you," he said fondly.

"No, I suppose I'm being silly," she said with a shaky laugh. She looked around the room, which now seemed perfectly normal. The air no longer vibrated with a sense of menace—she could easily have imagined the whole thing.

"Let's go," Corrado urged. "This place has been deserted so long that it's depressing. I'll take you home."

"No," she said determinedly. "I'm not ready to go home yet. You promised to help me today."

"But where else do you want to go?"

"Into Naples. Show me the fishing quarter where you lived with your family. I want to see the places I used to know. Please, Corrado. Perhaps something will come back to me there."

"All right." He drew her from the room and out of the house. In a moment he'd swung the car back onto the road, and soon they were engulfed by the city. Philippa's first thought was that she'd arrived in bedlam. Naples had been built between the sea and the hills, leaving nowhere to expand, so that a growing population had squeezed itself somehow into the existing space. In this quarter the streets were narrow, steeply sloping and paved with flagstones. Fruit and flower stalls stood on each side, making the space even more confined. Customers bargained at the tops of their voices, occasionally pausing to hop out of the way of the traffic. There were few traffic lights to inhibit the gladiatorial spirits of the drivers, and anyone wanting to cross took a deep breath and made a run for it.

The buildings were four and five stories high, connected by lines of washing. Dozens of windows stood open, each one bounded by a small iron balcony decorated with pots of flowers. The din was deafening but cheerful. And over it all hung the special scent of Naples, made up of fruit, vegetables, oil, spices and the sea.

A change had come over Corrado. He was driving with a verve and exhilaration that matched the company around him. It was the first time Philippa had seen his reserved exterior fall away with anyone but herself, and she watched in fascination as he swerved sharply to avoid another vehicle that had tried to cut in front of him, swiftly maneuvered ahead again and exchanged ritual pleasantries with the other driver. He gave her a quick glance when he heard her laughing and said ruefully, "I'm still a Neapolitan."

"So am I," Philippa said impulsively. Another facet of herself was becoming clear to her. She was instantly at home among these colorful, boisterous people with their dark beauty, violent gestures and singsong speech. Something robust and vibrant in herself acknowledged fellowship. Or perhaps, she thought, it was the echo of a childhood spent among them.

"Let's have coffee," Corrado said, and darted into a parking space that had just opened up outside a café. He made it under the nose of another driver who'd had his eye on the same space, murmuring, "The race is to the swift."

His defeated opponent seemed to disagree with this point of view. He stood up in his open car and directed a stream of colorful vituperation at Corrado, who grinned. Then his face brightened and he yelled, "Paolo!"

The other man beamed with joy. "Corrado, you son-of-a—" The rest was lost in the honking of horns around them.

As they got out of the car Corrado said to Philippa, "He's the cousin whose picture you saw yesterday, a bit brash but a good fellow at heart. He wasn't at our wedding."

Paolo managed to park on the other side of the road, jumped out and ran to clap Corrado on the back. He was a large, bearlike man, with a broad smile and a deafening voice. "You swindler!" he roared, beaming. "You deserve a beating for that."

"Another time, Paolo," Corrado said, grinning and fending him off. "Meet my wife instead."

Paolo clasped Philippa's hand in his two great paws. "Sorry I couldn't make the wedding."

"He didn't come because he was away making money," Corrado explained. "Paolo's becoming a great man."

"Great enough to buy you coffee to show I forgive you that underhanded trick you just played," Paolo announced, sweeping them inside the café.

He identified Philippa easily as "that skinny little kid who wanted to be more Neapolitan than the Neapolitans," but she soon realized that she wouldn't discover much through Paolo. He was much too self-absorbed. If he'd heard any rumors about Philippa he would have forgotten them within minutes.

Over their snack he boasted happily about the fleet he'd built up. "You wouldn't guess I was the same man as the one you used to know," he told Philippa. "I started from nothing, with just one boat plus that little dinghy you liked so much."

"You mean *The Swallow*?" she asked, thinking of the boat in the picture. "It was blue and the name was painted on in yellow."

Paolo grinned at her words. "Fancy you still remembering that."

"I had some very happy times in that boat," she ventured.

"I'll say. You never seemed to get enough of the sea. You made Corrado teach you everything he knew about sailing. D'you know, I still have that boat."

"I'm glad. I'd love to see it again."

"Nothing easier," Paolo boomed. "I was on my way down to the quay to inspect a new trawler I've just bought. You two come with me, eh?"

"Yes," Philippa said immediately, looking at Corrado expectantly.

"Of course," he agreed.

The smell of the ocean became stronger as they drove down to the quay, and Philippa took in great breaths of the tangy air. Paolo had said she was a true Neapolitan because the sea called to her, and the tingling excitement in her blood told her he was right.

Then Corrado had maneuvered out of a side street, and the whole glory of the bay of Naples was before her. The great curved expanse of water shimmered under the midday sun, its deep, almost impossible blue reflecting the cloudless sky. Philippa gasped at the sight. "It hasn't changed," Corrado said, glancing at her and smiling. "It's just as it was when you left eight years ago."

"And I've never seen it since?" she said incredulously. "How could I bear to stay away?"

Corrado didn't answer, and she became too preoccupied with the sights to notice the sadness that had settled on his face. When he spoke again it was neutrally. "We're nearly there."

They followed Paolo and spent some minutes dutifully admiring what he assured them was the foundation of the greatest fishing fleet in Naples. But at last he relented and led them to where a small blue dinghy bobbed in the water. Philippa recognized it at once from the photograph. She tried to picture herself as an eager fifteen-year-old, running along the quay, longing for the hours ahead when she would have Corrado to herself in a boat that was only large enough for two.

"I've kept her in good shape," Paolo explained, "and used her to teach my children to sail. But they've gone on to bigger things now, so I suppose her days are numbered. She'll make good firewood."

Out of the corner of his eye Corrado saw Philippa's instinctive movement of protest, but before she could speak he casually said, "There's no need for that. I'll buy her."

Paolo laughed. "But she's worthless. You could buy a hundred better boats."

"I want that one."

"But what could you do with it?"

"Give it to my wife," Corrado said.

"Ah, if you want to buy your wife a boat—"

"I want to buy her *that* boat," Corrado insisted quietly. He was looking at Philippa. She met his gaze, but her eyes were blurred by sudden tears at Corrado's understanding. She turned away to dry them surreptitiously, and when she looked back Corrado was writing Paolo a check.

"How did you know?" she asked huskily after they'd exchanged farewells with Paolo.

"I suppose I'm beginning to know you," he said wryly. "Shall I show you over your property?"

He boarded first and reached up to take her hand. The boat rocked madly, but although she couldn't recall sailing before she didn't feel at all uneasy. This was right. Everything about it felt right. Her body had done these things even if her mind didn't know it, and she followed her instincts, resisting Corrado's attempts to ease her toward the bow. "I wonder if you know why you chose that end," he said when she'd seated herself in the stern.

"Did I sit here in the past?"

"Always. After I'd showed you how to work the tiller you couldn't keep away from it."

"Why don't we see how much I can remember?"

"Now?"

"There'll never be a better time."

"All right," he said after a moment's hesitation. "There isn't much wind, but then you always had a talent for—" He checked himself.

"For what?" Philippa demanded.

"Let's see if you remember when we get out there." His eyes gleamed as he added provocatively. "If you make any mistakes I can always take over."

"You know what you can do with that idea," she said merrily.

Corrado laughed and began to haul the sail. By the time it was up, Philippa had dropped the rudder down into the water, tested the direction of the breeze and adjusted her position so that she was sitting with her back to it. The boom swung toward her, and she instinctively reached out to catch the rope attached to its end. Then she paused in confusion. "This rope..." she said hesitantly.

"It's called a sheet," Corrado told her. "You pass it through the sheet horse, which is that metal rail on the stern just behind you."

She was already performing the actions before he'd finished. The names meant nothing to her, but the movements came back to her almost immediately. She pulled on the sheet and felt it strain against the sheet horse, giving her control of the sail. "All right, let's go," Corrado said.

She cast off the stern line and pulled on the tiller. The little boat changed angle just enough to catch the first puff of wind. The sail filled, hauling on the sheet, trying to wrench it from her hand. At once she tightened her grip, leaning back to counter the unbalancing effect of the wind.

Corrado sat in the bow and watched her deftly manipulate the tiller and the sheet, increasing the angle to the wind until they picked up a sudden burst of speed. She was frowning with concentration.

After ten minutes they'd left the shore well behind. Without warning the wind strengthened, tilting the boat too much, so that her body's weight was no longer enough to balance it. Corrado shifted to sit on the gunwale to add his weight to hers, but she stopped him with a shake of her head, allowing the sheet to run through her hand until she'd settled the sail at an angle that offered less wind resistance and moving the tiller to leeward. She managed everything in one easy, fluid movement, and a glow broke over her face as she felt the boat straighten. She could have cried aloud with joy.

Flushed with triumph, she looked up, and her eyes met Corrado's. He was smiling tenderly. "Now I'll tell you," he said. "You always had a talent for getting every last puff of wind—you still have it, Philippa."

The light danced and sparkled on the water, throwing everything into dazzling relief. She feasted her eyes on him, sitting there, his hair ruffled by the breeze, the harsh yet strangely gentle lines of his face given a new vividness by the brilliant sun. Her heart almost stopped as she was assailed by a feeling of bittersweet joy. Passion and yearning tenderness surged through her, and she was again the young girl looking at the man who filled the world for her.

But is that all it is? she wondered. Did I only love him then, or do I love him now?

The wild leap of her senses as she remembered his kiss was a kind of answer. So was the slow thunder of her heart at the thought of touching him again. Last night he'd kissed her with deliberate seductive intent, but only because he'd been trying to dominate her. He hadn't succeeded, but he'd roused a storm in her body that only he could quiet. The teenage Philippa no longer existed. She was a woman now, and it was as a woman that she wanted him. Sooner or later the battle of wills between them must be fought out to the finish, with one of them the victor. Almost unconsciously she tightened her hand on the tiller, and the boat turned.

"Where are we going?" Corrado asked after a while.

"I thought we'd try that little island over there," she said, pointing over his shoulder to where a rock formation had reared up out of the sea. It was sheer all the way around except for one tiny bay that her sharp eyes had spotted.

Corrado twisted to see, and when he turned back to her a strange look had come over his face. "Why did you choose that?" he asked.

"I didn't. I hardly realized it was there until I'd turned and it came into my sights. It was pure chance... *wasn't it*?"

The last words burst from her as she saw the intensity of his expression deepen. He didn't reply, but shook his head.

The mass of rocks was very close now, and Philippa could see that it would need a careful maneuver to get into the narrow bay. Her mind was in a fever of excitement from what she'd just heard, and she moved mechanically, not even aware that she was bringing up the boat in perfect style as she turned head-to-wind, put the helm down hard and swung through a tight 180-degree turn, releasing the sheet. They'd reached shallow water, and while Corrado lowered the sail she rolled up her trousers to jump over the side. Together they hauled *The Swallow* up the beach.

"Why did you shake your head that way?" she asked urgently. "Isn't it chance that made me head to this place? Have we ever been here before?"

"Once, long ago."

She looked around at the cove of yellow sand, enclosed on three sides by sheer rock. One side was broken by the mouth of a cave, but apart from that the rock presented a smooth surface, impossible to climb. The only way off the beach was by the sea. It was a place where lovers could come and be sure of privacy, but she and Corrado hadn't been lovers in those far-off days. All the love had been on her side. "Was it my idea to come here before?"

"That's one way of putting it. We were out sailing. I'd just told you that it would be our last lesson. Before I knew where I was, you'd turned the boat and we were headed here." He smiled. "You virtually kidnapped me. You were always very decisive about what you wanted."

"And I wanted you, didn't I? I brought you here because when I was fifteen I was in love with you."

"You imagined you were. You had a child's crush on me, that's all."

"What did I do, Corrado? Please tell me."

He reddened slightly. "You asked me to kiss you."

"And did you?"

"Only on the forehead. You thought of yourself as a seductive siren, but you were only a young girl. It would have been disgraceful to take advantage of you."

Suddenly it was as though the bright sun had gone in, and she was standing in a chill, cold light, swept by the misery of rejection as she had been on that long-ago day. "And besides, you were in love with Maria, weren't you?" she asked softly. "Perhaps you still are?"

"Of course I'm not. That died long ago. I began to see the truth about Maria when she so easily left me for a richer man."

"That's not what she says. According to her, your pride forced you to break the engagement. You wanted to shower her with diamonds—"

"Did I? Well, perhaps I said something of the kind then. But I didn't give her up in a fit of nobility, whatever she may have told you. She dropped me cold when—" He stopped suddenly.

"When what?"

"When she realized I wasn't going to make a fortune," he said quickly. "Philippa, please be sensible. You must have seen what she's like. You should have told me what she said, not let it bother you all this time."

"I tried to believe she was lying, but it all sounded so horribly plausible, especially when she said you laughed at me."

"She said that?" Corrado's eyes kindled.

" 'The gawky pest,' that's what you called me, according to her. And I must have been a pest, I can see that. Always bothering you and getting in the way when you wanted to be alone with her. Perhaps you'd have told me to beat it if you hadn't worked for my father—"

"That's another of Maria's charming little suggestions, I take it. Listen, if you weren't so confused and vulnerable, Maria's real motives would be as plain as day to you. In a funny way she was jealous of you, even then. I couldn't understand it because you were just a kid. But I think now she couldn't bear to share my attention. She's the one who thought you were a pest, but I knew you were a delightful person, generous and openhearted. I used to envy the man you'd really love when you grew up."

He left the words with their unspoken question hanging in the air between them. In the silence Philippa reached up and drew his head slowly down. She caressed him subtly with her kisses, enjoying the shock she could feel in his body. "I've grown up now," she whispered.

"Philippa," he said softly, half in plea, half in surrender.

She linked her hands behind his head and spoke to him so sweetly it made him tremble. "I've grown up. You said yourself I'd chosen my own time, and this is the time I choose. I don't understand what's happening, but I know that it's part of what happened eight years ago. I loved you then and I love you now. You were always mine, Corrado..." She pressed her lips against his, whispering, "And now I've come back to claim you."

Six

As she gently caressed his lips with her own, Corrado felt the last of his resistance drain away. His conscience had driven him to fight her resolutely, but he had no strength left. The desire he'd repressed too long surged up against the barriers of his self-control, flattened them and swept onward in an unstoppable flood. His arms seemed to find their own way around her, and when he tightened them her head fell back against his shoulder as though it belonged there. He stayed for a long time gazing down at her beautiful face, aching at how defenseless she looked. But he knew he was just as defenseless himself, caught in her spell.

He kissed her slowly. Now that he was no longer fighting her he was free to discover her at leisure. She tasted of spice and ripe corn, wine and fresh spring-water, bread and honey and every good thing of the earth. She was manna falling to the desert to nourish his hungry senses and even hungrier spirit.

No woman had ever tormented him as she did, driving him frantic with the need to touch her, yet keeping him at bay by her innocence even while she lured him on. At last he could allow himself to taste the forbidden fruit, and it was a thousand times sweeter than in his dreams. A groan was wrenched from him as he felt her slim body tremble in his arms and press intimately against him.

The sound went through Philippa and mingled with the tremors that shook her. The blood was pounding in her veins, and she was flooded with joy as she realized that, for the first time, Corrado wasn't resisting her, but giving himself up to the feelings she could arouse in him.

Everything was different from their other encounters. He had a new purposefulness as he kissed her, teasing and assaulting her seductively until her lips parted. He immediately took her lower lip gently between his teeth and played his tongue skillfully against it. With every light touch her excitement mounted, until her toes curled at the overwhelming sensation. If he could do that to her with only a light kiss, what would it be like when he claimed her completely? She felt the warmth between her thighs and the sweet-sharp fever of anticipation and wondered if he knew he was sending her out of her mind.

He explored her mouth leisurely. He was going slowly, not yet committed past recall, giving her time to draw back. But all the time the flickering forays of his tongue tempted her on to sweet delight, and she couldn't have drawn back if her life had depended on it. She wanted him in all the different ways a woman can want a man, and she let her body tell him this, for she discovered it knew a mysterious and subtle language of its own.

He'd encompassed one breast in a large, powerful hand. The movements of his fingers were gentle, but they had an expertise that sent pleasurable torment flooding through her. "You were only a girl when you left me," he murmured huskily, "but I knew...one day...one day..."

"Yes...what did you know?" she asked eagerly.

He answered not in words, but by sweeping her up in his arms and carrying her toward the cave. Philippa understood the silent message. Once, in another life, they'd both known that at last this moment would come for them.

She clung to him, both arms around his neck, looking up, trying to read his expression. His face was dark with desire, his lips parted. She could hear the slight rasping sound of his breath and feel his chest rising and falling against her breasts. She was dizzy at the thought of the coming union, and she knew it was the same with him. He looked like a man lost in a dream.

It was cool inside the cave. The heat of Corrado's body was close to hers, and the thunder of his heart was in time with her own. He laid her gently on the firm sand and immediately drew her against him, kissing her face again and again. "I tried so hard to resist you," he said hoarsely, "but it's no use."

"No," she murmured as she felt his tongue caress the sensitive place below her ear. "This was meant to happen. I may not know anything else, but I know that."

He teased her with seductive kisses along the length of her neck, until he came to rest at the base of her throat. Without moving his mouth he reached for the buttons of her shirt. When the last one was open he pulled the shirt from her waistband, then eased it off, revealing an expanse of pale, silky skin. The feel of his hand on her was unbearably good, and Philippa moaned softly, arching against him so that he could move his fingers freely around to her back.

He unhooked the clasp of her bra and drew the tiny garment forward. Philippa didn't see where it fell. Her whole attention was concentrated on Corrado, watching him as he saw her naked breasts for the first time. It mattered so much that he should find her beautiful.

At first she couldn't believe what she saw, but then she understood. He was gazing at her with a kind of incredulous wonder, as though afraid to accept the evidence of his own eyes. Suddenly he began to move quickly, tearing open the buttons of his shirt and throwing it off, then seizing her in his arms and crushing her against him. Forked lightning went through her as the wiry hair on his chest rasped against her delicate skin. "Am I too rough for you?" he whispered into her tousled hair.

"No," she breathed, reveling in the contact with him. She moved her hands over him, feeling the muscular outline of his body, discovering with wonder that this powerful man was trembling in her arms.

"Philippa..." he said tensely. "You have to be sure. If you have any doubts—we can still turn back—but not for much longer."

"We *can't* turn back," she said deliriously. "It's too late. You belong to me—as I belong to you. You want me, I can feel it."

"If you knew how much I've wanted you, Philippa...for so long. I couldn't rush you...it had to be right."

"It *is* right," she told him. "This was always meant to happen." She was working on him as she spoke, demonstrating the witchery that somehow she possessed. There was genius in her fingers. They seemed to know of their own accord how to touch him and elicit the mysterious vibrations of physical harmony.

"Yes," he murmured, "yes...that's how it should be."

"How does it feel?"

"Wonderful," he groaned. "Nothing has ever been like it." A faint gleam of humor shone in his eyes. "Let me see if I can make you feel as wonderful."

He slid one hand around her until he reached her spine and began to play along it with his fingers. Philippa let out a long sigh of pleasure. As he caressed her he easily opened and removed her trousers. Her stockings followed, leaving her in nothing but the minute panties that hardly covered her at all. She lifted her hand to remove them but he stopped her. "I'll do that," he said quietly.

She smiled with pleasure at their mutual understanding. She wanted Corrado to undress her, as though by that possessive act he signified that she belonged to him. She wanted to feel his fingers curling around the edge of the lacy material, as they were doing now, sliding over her hips and down her long, slender legs.

She lay there while he devoured her with his eyes. "You're so lovely," he said huskily, "almost too perfect to be touched."

But every inch of her ached to feel his caresses, and she reached up for him. Corrado dropped his head and laid it between her breasts, pressing his face into the soft fullness. He took one rosy nipple between his lips and played with it gently. A tide of joy swept through her newly awakened body. She'd desired Corrado before this, but that desire had given her only the faintest premonition of the craving that would rage through her when at last she was with him, close to the moment of union, her flesh burning to receive his love.

Philippa writhed in his arms, moaning softly at the artistry of his tongue, which teased the nipple into a hard peak. A sensual storm had been unleashed within her, and only Corrado could quell it. She ran her fingers through his black hair again and again, repeating his name mindlessly, letting him know her impatience.

He tore at his belt and ripped open his trousers. He removed them in a moment and gathered her into his arms again, possessed by his own explosive need. Philippa parted her legs and felt him there, probing her gently, then insistently, and finally entering her with controlled power.

At the feel of him inside her she cried out with ecstasy. Everything in her welcomed him. She looked up through hazy eyes to see him watching her anxiously. "Are you all right?" he asked softly. "I don't want to hurt you?"

"You couldn't. I want everything we can have together."

"We can have everything," he promised, smiling tenderly. "But let's take it slowly, my darling. This is new to you."

She could sense that he was right, and there was happiness in that discovery. Her surrender to Corrado was complete. She wanted to absorb him into her being and become one with him in another dimension where there was no unknown past, no mysterious future and no unanswered questions—only each other.

She was being driven by a primitive need that made her open body and heart to him and respond eagerly to his every move. Each thrust was as if he'd pierced her with joy, but a new kind of joy that illuminated the world, changing all her perspectives. She'd found the only reality that mattered.

She trembled as the pleasure mounted, carrying her into the white heat of the furnace so that she cried out and clung to him, feeling her inner self disintegrate, only to be gloriously recreated. Her past was very close now. That other Philippa, the lonely girl who'd yearned hopelessly for this man, seemed to be there, sharing at last in the happiness that had been denied her.

She became gradually aware of the distant roar of the sea. She was lying with her head against Corrado's chest, listening to his heartbeat slowing. "I must have been dreaming for eight years of making love with you," she whispered.

He tightened the arm around her, drawing her more closely to him. "But you became engaged to another man," he reminded her gently.

"But I never made love with him. I know that now. And you were the reason. I've loved you all this time."

"You won't know that until your memory returns."

"No, that's not true. There are some things you know with your heart, not your mind. You've been in my heart forever, and one day I was bound to come back to find you." She kissed him. "And now I have. I'm not going to lose you a second time. We're properly married. It's too late for an annulment. We can go ahead with the church service."

He was silent so long that a cold hand clutched her heart, and she sat up to look at him. "If that's all true, why did you run away from me on our wedding day?" he asked quietly.

In her happiness she'd forgotten all about that. Now it seemed like a story heard long ago. "It doesn't matter," she insisted. "That was another time. *I love you.* That won't change, whatever happens. If you don't love me, why don't you just tell me?"

Corrado sat up and took her face between his hands. "I do love you, Philippa," he said soberly. "I love you more than I ever believed I could love a woman. When I awake in the morning and know I'm going to see you, the sun comes out for me. I watch for your smile. I study your face when you're sad. I want to take you in my arms and protect you from the world, but I know you don't want my protection, and that's the hardest thing of all to bear.

"Your happiness means all the world to me. For the sake of that I'll risk everything I possess or hope for. I could even—" his voice shook slightly "—I could even let you go if it was for your good. That's how much I love you."

She couldn't speak. There'd been a depth of emotion in Corrado's voice that made an ache come to her throat and unshed tears blur her eyes. He saw the tears and kissed them away, understanding their cause. "But I want you to know that that's true," he said huskily. "You must be certain in your heart that I'm marrying you for love alone."

At last she managed to steady her voice enough to speak. "Why should I doubt that? Because of my money? It didn't trouble you when I signed a marriage settlement giving it all to you."

"I never asked for that settlement. It was your idea. You insisted on giving me everything, but I don't want it. As I told you this morning, I'll keep a protective eye on the firm while it's in my control, but I have no intention of touching the income."

"I know. I realized you weren't using it last night when you were talking to Giorgio. I also heard the way you made him read the small print of the contract, but you don't have to deal with me the same way. I'm a woman who loves you, not a business machine computing the terms. Don't let my money come between us, Corrado. It isn't my fault I have it."

She only half noticed the wry smile that flickered across his face. She was too preoccupied by the need to climb the invisible barrier that still separated them to think of anything else. "No, it's not your fault," he agreed. Then, to her surprise, he pulled her back into his arms in a gesture of passionate protection. "It's not your fault," he repeated.

"Then we won't allow it to make any difference. If we love each other, that's all that matters."

He sighed. "I meant to be so strong. I was going to keep you at a safe distance—"

She laughed and kissed him. "You'll never be safe from me, darling."

A sharp breeze was rising as they set sail again, making their return trip faster than the outward one. Philippa let Corrado take the tiller this time so that she could enjoy sitting in the bow and feasting her eyes on him.

Once in the car she sat twisted in her seat, still gazing at him as he drove. In the distance the sun was beginning to sink, flooding the land with deep golden light and illuminating Corrado's profile. Now and then he glanced at her and a faint smile played around his mouth. On a quiet stretch of road he removed a hand from the wheel and took hers, holding it for miles. Neither of them spoke. They'd found each other on a level where no words were needed. Philippa wondered if there'd ever been a time in the past when she was as perfectly, blissfully happy as she was now. She doubted it.

It was twilight when they drew up outside the house. "Don Ferrando's here," Corrado observed, noting the priest's battered car parked by the step.

They found Don Ferrando inside enjoying a glass of wine and some gossip with Anna. He rose when they entered and greeted Philippa with smiling courtesy while his gaze seemed to go through her. She was suddenly self-conscious. Beneath his charm the old man was a shrewd judge of people, and his bright eyes saw everything. She felt herself blushing at the conviction that Corrado's loving must be evident in every line of her glowing body.

"I've been telling Don Ferrando he works too hard," Anna declared, pouring wine for everyone.

"But at this time of year it's the pleasantest kind of work," he replied. "Lots of weddings. Everyone wants to be married in the summer." He chuckled. "The brides know how the sun shows off their wedding dresses." His eyes flickered between the two of them.

"Of course they do," Philippa agreed. "And it's about time my wedding dress had an airing. Corrado and I were going to come and see you tomorrow anyway about setting the date."

"That's splendid," the old man said, beaming at them both.

"So why don't we set it now?" she finished.

She saw from Corrado's face that he was taken aback by her decisive move. For a disconcerting moment it was as if he were conveying a silent message of caution, but she brushed the thought aside. She loved him, and every instinct, every fiber of her being told her that he loved her in return. What she'd seen in his eyes and what she'd sensed in the passionate possessiveness of his caresses were things that couldn't be faked. She must act quickly to make him her own.

Don Ferrando was thumbing through his diary. At last he named a date ten days hence. "The sooner the better," Philippa said, smiling up at Corrado. "Isn't that true?"

"Perfectly true," he agreed.

Delighted, the old man scribbled in the diary, drank another glass to their health and bustled out. A few moments later they heard him drive away. Philippa saw Corrado looking at her in exasperation and burst out laughing at the sight of his face. "It was a shocking and unprincipled thing to do, wasn't it?" she asked, putting her arms around him.

"Totally."

"I had you backed into a corner, and I made use of it in the most disgraceful fashion. After all, you could hardly turn me down in front of Don Ferrando. I'm sorry, darling. You'll just have to be resigned to a shotgun wedding."

He looked down into her flushed, happy face, and something went through his heart. "Philippa," he said gently. "Calm down. A little victory is a dangerous thing."

"It's not a little victory, it's a big victory. I've won the most important thing in the world. And don't tell me again that I don't know what's important to me, because I *do* know."

"All right, I won't say it. You know I wanted to wait until your memory returned before you commit yourself to me irrevocably, but I have no strength left to fight you. You've defeated me with my own love for you. Oh, Philippa..." The words were torn from him as he gathered her into his arms. "You've been very hasty," he said somberly, his lips against her tousled hair. "But I promise you, if it's in my power, I'll see that you never regret what you've just done."

"How could I?" she asked blissfully. "If we love each other, why should we ever regret showing that to the world?" She felt him kiss the top of her head, but he didn't answer.

Philippa was becoming lost again in the dark scent of him that pervaded her, bringing with it memories that made her dizzy with their potency. It was only a few hours since she'd lain beneath him, quivering with rapture while he possessed her body as completely as he'd possessed her heart. Yet already that was a lifetime ago. She was like a traveler in a new land, eagerly exploring uncharted terrain, untroubled by the lack of maps and relying on her instincts to bring her to the place where she belonged.

The haunting evocation of past delight was causing her body to heat, grow softer and mold itself to his contours. "As long as we have each other..." she said softly, looking up at him.

"Yes," he said thickly, speaking as if in a daze. "We have each other."

She could feel his hard arousal pressed against her through his trousers. "It's so long since you made love to me, Corrado," she whispered, adding with a provocative smile, "but perhaps you're tired now."

"You cunning, scheming little—" He growled the words out between kisses, which he rained over her face, and the last word of all was lost as he covered her mouth with his own. He was gasping when he finally tore his lips away. "Tired, am I? Shall I give you a demonstration of how tired I am?"

"Yes, please," she said promptly.

"We'll see who's tired when I'm through. I want to take and take from you, Philippa. I want to take all of your sweetness and your young, fierce passion that's as unspoiled as the world's dawn. And I want to give to you until you die inside from too much pleasure and understand how a man can really love a woman."

"Yes," she said against his mouth.

In her bedroom he undressed her again, almost fearfully, as though he were afraid to discover her less lovely than he remembered. But when she was naked his glowing eyes told her the truth, that for him, as for her, the reality was sweeter than any dream. He took her tenderly into his arms and loved her. Philippa gave herself up to him with joy, feeling her being flow into his, letting him lead her down paths of new delights, until at last the miracle was given back to her.

Seven

The next few days ran together in a continuous golden stream. Bathed in Corrado's love, Philippa was totally happy and without fear for the future.

She spent her nights in his arms, discovering him and offering the revelation of herself. They fulfilled and completed each other until their mutual hunger was briefly assuaged, slept the sleep of exhaustion only to wake and find the hunger more devouring than before. Each day the power that united them became stronger, until the rest of the world faded from sight, hidden by the glory they shared.

While Corrado was at the factory, Philippa concentrated on recovering her skills with pen and ink. She sketched the view of Vesuvius, at first tentatively, then with growing confidence and was delighted at how easily her hand recalled the expert movements.

She began to roam the countryside seeking out picturesque villages with baking walls and red-brown shutters closed against the midday sun.

She tried drawing Corrado, but discovered that she had no gift for portraits. He returned one day to find her sitting by the window in her room, contemplating the image on the pad. "Good lord, who's that?" he exclaimed.

"It's supposed to be you," she said defensively.

He began to laugh. She glared at him, offended, until she realized that she'd never seen him like this before, abandoning himself to genuine mirth. It made him seem years younger. A spring of happiness welled up inside her. "I'm sorry," he said. "I didn't mean to laugh, but if I thought I looked like that I'd shoot myself."

"If you looked like that *I'd* shoot you," she said, beginning to laugh too. She tossed the sketch pad away and threw herself into his arms. He kissed her exuberantly and fell onto the bed, taking her with him. "I like to hear you laugh," she said when she could speak again. "You hardly ever do."

"You've taught me to laugh again, *piccina mia*," he said. "I didn't know a man could be so happy."

"And we'll always be this happy, won't we?"

"Always," he said fiercely, tightening his arms around her until she was almost breathless. "Nothing's going to spoil our love, I swear it." His voice grew husky and took on a tone that always thrilled her. "Philippa..."

"Anna will be calling us for dinner in a minute," she murmured.

"Let her. We won't hear."

When they went down an hour later Anna met them on the terrace. "Your mother called today, *signore*. She wants you to call back."

He went to make the call, and Philippa took her place at the table. The message had made her a little apprehensive. Corrado's mother had been present on the night she ran away, but she'd returned home during Philippa's convalescence and they hadn't seen each other. Soon they would have to meet, as the older woman would naturally come to the church service.

She looked up quickly as Corrado reappeared. "Mama wants me to take you to visit her in Pozzuoli," he said. "She says it's better if you don't meet in a crowd on the wedding day. She's right."

"Is she offended that we haven't been to visit earlier?"

He shook his head. "I'd told her about your amnesia, and she agreed with me that, until you were fully recovered we should spare you the strain of being with people you knew but couldn't remember." He covered her hand with his own. "Don't worry, *piccina*. My mother is a very understanding woman, and she was always fond of you."

"I don't see how she can be fond of me after the way I deserted you on our wedding day."

"Mama makes her own judgments according to her own rules. You can ask her about it yourself. I said we'd go tomorrow. Do you mind?"

"No, of course not. I'm just being silly."

They left early the next day. Pozzuoli was to the west of Naples, and Corrado drove along the magnificent Via Posillipo. "It's breathtaking, isn't it?" he said, as Philippa gasped at the series of gorgeous palaces that lined one side of the road, looking out onto the sea. "At one time this was the fashionable quarter, and anyone who was anyone came here for the winter—Virgil, Tiberius, Nero." He stopped the car. "Can you hear anything?"

"Yes," she said after a moment. "There's a strange noise coming from far below, a sort of roaring moan. It sounds eerie."

"It should. It's the wailing of Queen Giovanna's lovers. She liked handsome fishermen, and when she'd had her way with them she ordered them to be drowned, thus proving that the female really is deadlier than the male. You can still hear their moans along this coast."

Philippa laughed. "What is it really?"

"The rocks below form cavernous vaults along the shoreline. When the sea washes into them it makes that noise." He started the car again. "This part of the world is full of legends, not only because of the sea, but because of the volcanoes. There are so many craters around here that the Romans thought it was the mouth of hell. One of them still has mud and sulfur boiling away."

"Is it safe for your mother to live here, then?"

"I don't like it," Corrado said. "But she was born in Pozzuoli, and she's insisted on going back to live in the same house. She says she needs to see the sea when she gets up in the morning. As for the future . . ." He shrugged. "She's a fatalist."

For most of the way the road hugged the coast. Then they were driving the last half mile to the entrance to the town, and suddenly Philippa turned and stared, riveted by an utterly astounding sight. An old building, half in ruin, rose directly out of the water. "It used to be a Capuchin monastery," Corrado said. "But the volcanoes have made the land so unstable that it's subsided under the water. On a clear day you can take a boat out and look down at the docks that the Romans built here two thousand years ago."

He drove slowly along the quay, which was lined by small houses. Most of the front doors were open, and elderly people sat just outside, talking or mending fishing nets. Some of them waved to Corrado. "I'll swear this place hasn't changed since I was a boy," he said.

His mother came from the same time warp. The Greeks who'd colonized this part of the world before the Romans, many centuries ago, had left an enduring legacy. Rosa Bennoni had a stately Greek beauty, which was still visible despite her years and her brown, weather-beaten skin, and which was emphasized by her height and air of proud calm, as if she embodied all the wisdom of the ages. Her iron-gray hair was drawn back sleekly, revealing the fine shape of her head.

She embraced her son while Philippa hesitated in some confusion, wondering how to greet her. Corrado's mother solved the problem, coming forward with open arms and kissing her daughter-in-law on both cheeks. Then she stood back, her hands on Philippa's shoulders, and looked into her face. "Good," she said, as if she'd seen something that satisfied her. "Are you better now?"

"I'm quite recovered from the accident, but I'm afraid I..."

"You don't know me, eh? But I know you. Tell me, has a knock on the head ruined your appetite?"

"No," Philippa said, laughing.

"Good. Then come inside and eat. As a child you always loved my *zuppa di pesce*, so I made it for you specially."

Philippa felt her heart lift at this encouraging welcome, and soon she was sitting in the spotless little kitchen, drinking Lacrima Christi while Rosa ladled fish stew onto her plate. Of the numerous fish Philippa identified only prawns and mussels, bathed in a sauce that smelled of tomatoes, celery, garlic, melon and wine. Rosa set down a basket filled with hunks of brown bread and commanded, "Eat."

Philippa had been too nervous to take any breakfast beyond black coffee, but now her appetite came flooding back. She ate enthusiastically while Corrado and his mother talked, and she realized that she was being left in peace so that she could find her feet without hassle.

She cleared her plate and delighted Rosa by asking for more. Then there was fresh ripe fruit and delicious coffee. While they were drinking this the door opened, and another elderly woman, with a slight resemblance to Rosa, walked in. Corrado greeted her joyfully as Aunt Senta and introduced her to Philippa as Rosa's sister.

Aunt and nephew immediately became engaged in lively gossip that grew into an argument. They talked in rapid, pungent Neapolitan dialect. Philippa couldn't follow this unless it was spoken slowly, and she soon became lost. But it was clear that they were both growing heated, raising their voices to be heard over each other. Philippa stared at the sight of Corrado roaring at the old woman, but Senta was roaring back, giving as good as she received and plainly enjoying herself.

"Let's go where it's quiet," Rosa said, smiling while she led the way outside.

The beach stretched in both directions, cluttered with little boats. Men and women sat on or beside them, mending nets. One man puffed his pipe and silently contemplated a bucket full of starfish. He looked as if he could sit there forever, in the same pose as his ancestors.

It was a scene from another age, far removed from the turbulence of Philippa's own life, and even farther from the hectic bustle of the industrial empire she'd inherited. It was suddenly easy to believe that the stormy events of the last few weeks were no more than a speck on the surface of the ocean. The past and the future, both equally mysterious, would one day both be clear to her and fall into place in the long, flowing tide of her life. Impulsively she said, "How wonderfully peaceful this is."

"Yes," Rosa agreed, her mind still on the uproar they'd left. "But you don't want to worry about those two. They've always enjoyed a good shouting match. Many times when you were younger you'd laugh when they started one of their arguments. But of course, you don't remember that."

"Not a thing," Philippa said regretfully. "I wish I did."

"You're not ready," Rosa said. "When you *are* ready, you'll remember. Very simple." She shrugged. "Life is simple if you take it the right way."

"But what is the right way?"

"Listen to your heart's wisdom. It's only the brain that forgets. The heart remembers to the end."

"My heart tells me that I love Corrado and want to be with him always, no matter what—" She hesitated.

"No matter what you find out?" Rosa finished for her.

"Yes," Philippa agreed resolutely. "No matter what I find out. I only wish my heart would tell me why I ran from him on our wedding day."

She watched Rosa as she spoke these words to see if she could detect a clue or a hint of condemnation. But her mother-in-law only shook her head. "The time wasn't right for your marriage," she said calmly. "Now it is."

"But it was only a few weeks ago."

"It's not days and weeks that count, or even years. It's how you change inside." Rosa smiled. "I can remember a young girl who came to our house years ago, and I saw she loved my son with a true and honest heart. I was sure you were the one for him."

"But he didn't see it, did he?"

"I think, with one part of him he did," Rosa answered slowly. "But he was blinded by that painted piece he was engaged to. I used to pray that he'd make the right choice before it was too late. Well . . . now he has. Not in the way I'd thought, but that doesn't matter. Things happen as they must."

"Corrado told me you were a fatalist," Philippa said, looking at the older woman with fascination.

"Of course. All fishing folk believe in fate, because that way we can live with death without looking over our shoulders." Rosa stretched her arm out in the direction of the ocean. "The sea is greedy. She doesn't give up anything if she can help it. For centuries we've watched our men take their boats out to fight her for a few miserable pounds of fish, and we know one day she might not let them come back. I never asked my husband not to go, because I knew he loved that cruel she-devil. He did what he had to, and one day she grew possessive and kept him with her.

"So I came here to live with my sister, whose husband died like mine. And my son says, 'Mama, don't live in that place. It's dangerous.' Hah! Much he knows!"

"Isn't it dangerous?"

Rosa gave a dismissive shrug. "Perhaps. Somewhere deep underground there are channels that connect Pozzuoli to Vesuvius. One day, one of us will go up. Maybe in fifty years. Maybe tomorrow."

"But you love it here, don't you?"

"Yes. I was happy here as a child. The past doesn't let go, Philippa, even for you, who think you don't know the past. At last I came back to where my heart was . . . just as you did."

"I was bound to come back to Corrado," Philippa said quickly. "I'm sure of that."

"Yes. I've watched you with him today, and I've seen the same look of adoration on your face that was there years ago."

"What about when I first arrived for the wedding?" Philippa asked. "Did you see it then?"

"No," Rosa said, smiling to herself. "You were very careful to hide it. But you can't hide love forever, any more than you can silence a volcano. It lies quiet until you think it's extinct, but one day it erupts without warning and engulfs you."

"Yes," Philippa said eagerly. "I've felt almost guilty because I have so much happiness when others have none." She drew a sharp breath, as though a cloud had shadowed her sunny confidence. "I wonder if I'll find I was living in a fool's paradise all the time," she added quietly.

"Better that than live in a fool's hell with no love," Rosa said, watching her face. "Don't feel guilty because you have love. Cherish it and build on it, so that when troubles come you'll be strong."

"What do you mean when you say I 'think' I don't know the past? I really don't know it."

"But you do," Rosa replied simply. "You've hidden the knowledge deep inside of yourself. When the moment is right, you'll know where to find it. But don't rush things. Corrado is very wise to make you take your time."

"I was hoping to learn something from you," Philippa said. "But I suppose you're under orders from Corrado."

"I take orders from no man," Rosa said crisply. "Still less from a boy I used to smack for leaving axle grease all over my clean floors. But Corrado must run his marriage for himself."

A bellow of exuberant laughter from within the house made Rosa smile. "You see? They're perfectly good friends." As if to prove it Corrado came out with his arm around Senta's shoulders.

"We shall meet again in a few days, when I come for your wedding," Rosa said, embracing Philippa warmly. "And this time you won't run away."

They drove home in the light of a crimson sunset. "Did my mother say anything interesting?" Corrado inquired casually.

Philippa chuckled. "Yes. She told me you used to leave axle grease on the floors!"

She found a letter from Aunt Claire waiting for her at home. Philippa had called her to invite her to the wedding, but her aunt couldn't make the trip. The older woman had tried hard to persuade her not to go ahead until her memory returned. Now she'd written, putting her plea more forcefully.

> You're crazy to go through with this in ignorance. You simply don't know what you might be getting into. You've always been this way, headstrong and blind to the pitfalls when you've set your heart on something. But I remember how often you came to grief....

Late at night Philippa took out the letter and read it again in her room. Her aunt's words troubled her, because they seemed to echo an unspoken message that had come from Rosa. Beneath the kindly encouragement Philippa had sensed that Rosa was preparing her for something that would test her love.

She heard movement on the other side of the connecting door and hastily dropped the letter into her purse just before Corrado came in, wearing only a pair of pajama trousers. She was swept by sudden fear, as if all she held most precious had been threatened by forces she couldn't control, and held out her arms to him. "Love me," she pleaded urgently.

Corrado heard the new note in her voice and crossed the room in two strides, dropping onto the bed beside her and gathering her into his arms. "What is it, *piccina mia*?" he whispered between kisses. "What's wrong?"

Instead of answering she clung to him tightly. She wanted to become submerged in him, engulfed by him, lost past recall, until there was no longer any "self" to be tormented by fears. "What's wrong?" he repeated.

"Nothing's wrong," she said. "Only... love me... always."

A tender smile played around his mouth. "Do you doubt my love still? Must I prove it to you again?" he asked.

Already she was turning to liquid flame inside. "Yes," she said softly.

Her heart was beating with anticipation. Every night spent in Corrado's arms had brought new revelations of his skills as a lover. She knew how he could hold her strongly but tenderly in his muscular arms, knew the control with which he could prolong their loving until she was almost out of her mind and the power with which he could thrust deeply into her, driving her into a delirium of ecstasy and fulfillment. The remembrance of these things was burned into her senses and her spirit, and now she was driven by the craving to experience them again.

He looked down at her as she lay in his arms, her breasts rising and falling as passion possessed her. Through the thin material of her nightgown he could see her nipples already peaked with anticipation. He dropped his head and drew his lips slowly across her neck and throat, relishing the silky perfection of her skin and its scent of warmth and arousal. Just breathing in that special perfume was enough to make his heart beat faster and to kindle his desire for her.

He pushed aside the material to reveal one pale, perfect breast. "You get more beautiful all the time," he said huskily. "How can any man be so lucky?" He was caressing her breast as he spoke, and Philippa moaned softly as a feeling of almost unbearable delight swept through her. "How shall I tell you that I love you?" he asked, his mouth against her soft flesh.

"Like that," she whispered, caught in a crazy spiral of feeling. "Yes, Corrado, like that."

His tongue was lazily circling the peaked nipple, sending a stream of shivering pleasure through her. Philippa ran her fingers through his hair, flexing them again and again. Sliding her hands lower, she could feel his broad, muscular back, tense and hard beneath her palms. His whole body had that same steely strength, and she comforted herself with the thought, as though it were a talisman to keep out everything that threatened their love. Here in his arms she knew she'd discovered her true self. Her life had begun only when she opened her eyes on Corrado's face.

He closed his lips purposefully on the peaked nipple and played with it before releasing it with an abrupt movement that sent delicious vibrations shuddering through her. She shifted so that he could treat the other nipple to the same sweet torment. He anticipated her wish and hastened to please her. It felt so good that a tremulous sob escaped her. "Oh, yes...oh, Corrado, I want you."

"And soon you'll want me more, *piccina*," he said thickly. "This is only the start. We have the whole night before us...the whole night for me to make you understand that you're mine."

"I think...I already know that," she managed to say.

He gave a slow smile. "Not as you will know it by morning," he promised.

He removed her nightgown with fevered hands, then stood up briefly to remove his pajama trousers. For Philippa this was always a moment of wonder as she saw the taut outlines of his hips and thighs, the firm buttocks and flat stomach and the uncompromising virility that told her of his passion more plainly than words.

He dropped beside her on the bed and clasped her to him, molding her against him. Philippa gasped at the tingling shock of that contact and arched so that his hair-roughened skin stimulated her again and again. Every line, every inch of his body was exciting to her. It was a thrilling, erotic instrument, attuned to take her through all the variations of sensual harmony.

The intimate pressure of his loins emphasized the urgency of his desire, and Philippa parted her legs in eager anticipation. But he delayed their most profound union while he embarked on a leisurely dalliance for her delight. He caressed her with his tongue, making teasing assaults on her soft skin wherever he knew her to be most sensitive. He'd quickly made himself an expert in her responses, and he used his expertise with the confidence of a man who knew he was the only possible lover for the woman in his arms.

He conquered her willing body with subtle power, as if he were someone reclaiming his own possession. He feasted his eyes on her as though discovering treasure, trying to take it all in at once, but confused by the abundance of riches. To the victor all things must be given, and this victor knew how to ask even as he plundered and to give back what he took a thousandfold.

He lavished kisses over her everywhere—her throat and breasts, the hollow of her tiny waist, the tender skin of her inner thighs, which was burningly sensitive and eager to receive him. Philippa surrendered to the dark, primitive magic with joyous, trusting acceptance. Her whole self was concentrated into a single flame of desire, which blazed higher with every moment that passed.

At last Corrado moved over her, and she offered herself to him without reserve. He entered her slowly, and she let out a long breath of satisfaction as she felt herself become whole. He slipped his hands beneath her, pulling her more closely to him while he lost himself in her again and again. She was caught up in a spiral of ecstasy that whirled her around dizzily. With every thrust the whirling grew faster.

The pleasure was mounting to heights she'd never dreamed of. She closed her thighs fiercely about him, silently entreating him never to let it end. They were possessed by a timeless force that carried them into a new world filled with fire and explosive joy. The light was blinding in its beauty. His name broke from her lips in a shuddering cry as the volcano swept them both away in a stream of molten gold.

Now there was only silence and the profound calm of fulfillment. Philippa lay against Corrado, her arms curled possessively about him. All doubts were stilled. It was as Rosa had said. The time was right, and her heart had come home to her love.

Eight

Rosa and Senta arrived the day before the wedding. They were followed by Paolo and his wife Martha. That evening Don Ferrando came, and the seven of them had a party on the terrace overlooking Naples. Philippa had expected this to be something of an ordeal, but found instead that she was enjoying herself. The priest had a fund of funny stories and a gift for mimicry that made every tale live. He also turned out to possess a fine baritone voice and entertained them with Neapolitan songs that were more than a little scandalous.

It must have been like this on the night she ran away. But now Philippa could find no trace of the doubt and fear that must have driven her then. She longed only for the next day to be over so that this limbo should end, and she would truly be Corrado's wife.

When Don Ferrando's car had clanked away into the night, and they'd seen their guests to bed, they said good-night to each other on the landing. "It's back to separate rooms tonight, I'm afraid," Corrado said with a sigh as he took her into his arms. "For my mother's sake we must at least appear to consider the proprieties."

"Shall I tell you how improper I really feel at this moment?" she asked, nestling against him.

"I think you'd better not," he said unsteadily. "My self-control is already stretched to the limit. If only it were tomorrow night."

"You can't wish that any more than I do," she assured him fervently.

While she spoke she caressed his chest and toyed with his shirt buttons. She succeeded in undoing one before he groaned and said, "Will you stop that, or do you want me to be a nervous wreck at the altar?" She laughed provocatively, and he pulled her close to blot out the tempting sight. "If I should lose you now..." he murmured against her lips.

"You'll never lose me," she told him between kisses. "Never...never...my love."

"Tell me that everything's all right—that you have no doubts."

"No doubts," she insisted. "I won't run away again."

"It isn't that. It's that I feel I'm doing wrong in letting you marry me like this. But I can't help it. I want you so much that it silences my conscience. But I wonder if you'll forgive me in the years to come."

"Hush." She laid a hand gently over his mouth. "Don't torment yourself uselessly. If we love each other, there can be no 'wrong,' no need for forgiveness."

"And if ever a man loved a woman, I love you," he said. "My darling, promise me that you'll never let yourself forget that."

"How absurd you're being. How can I ever forget it?"

"Promise," he insisted with an edge of desperation in his voice.

"Very well, I promise."

"Good night, my dearest."

She kissed him again and again. "Good night... good night," she whispered, "until tomorrow, Corrado."

He tore himself away from her and went to his room. Philippa waited until he was out of sight before opening her own door. Then she stopped, petrified.

In the moonlight she could see the figure of a man standing by the window. She put out her hand for the light switch, but he moved to intercept her. In a moment he'd pulled her into the room, shut the door and placed his finger over her lips. Angrily she pushed it aside, but found that he'd gotten between her and the door. "Hush," he said urgently. "I'm not here to hurt you. Surely you know who I am? Don't say you've forgotten me, darling."

"You have no right to call me 'darling,'" she said furiously. "Get away from that door."

The man flicked on the light. He was a large man in his mid-thirties, with brown hair and an edgy look about his face. "I'm not moving until I've told you all the things Corrado Bennoni has been carefully concealing," he said. "You really don't know me? Your aunt said you had amnesia, but I thought after all we've shared, all the love there's been between us . . . I'm Michael Radley." He watched comprehension dawn on her face and said wryly, "I see you've heard of me."

"Yes," she said slowly. She could identify him now as the man she'd been with in the picture from the engagement party. "We were engaged once."

"We're in love," he said emphatically.

"No!" Philippa flinched away from him. Her body was still singing with rapture from Corrado's kisses, and there was something brutally horrible about this stranger's confident assertion that she loved him. "That's impossible!" she told him frantically. "I'm sorry—I can see who you are, and I know we were engaged—but I *can't* believe I ever loved you." Nausea at the thought mingled with a nameless fear that was trying to batter its way into her mind.

"That's because you're not yourself," Michael said with such self-satisfaction that she shivered. "If you were in your right mind you'd know you love me, and what you imagine you feel for Bennoni is only an illusion—an illusion he's done everything in his power to foster."

Horror kept her petrified while Michael Radley continued. "I've been trying to get to see you for weeks, but Bennoni has kept you incommunicado. He even changed the phone number to stop me calling you because it suits his purpose for you to go on being half crazy. Tonight I broke in, because I had to tell you the truth in time to stop this wedding."

"You can't stop it," she burst out. "I love Corrado—"

"You don't love him. You're marrying him out of guilt. All he cares about is your money, and he played on your conscience to get it."

"Conscience?" she echoed. Images were chasing through her brain: the dream with herself pleading for forgiveness and Corrado saying that some wrongs could never be made right. Her mouth felt dry. "What do you mean, conscience?" she demanded.

"Your father made his fortune from a new electrical component. It revolutionized the industry. He invented it while he was living here, and Bennoni did some of the preliminary drawings under Edward's direction. He was just the hired help obeying orders, but on the strength of those drawings he tried to claim the rights. It was a desperate attempt to get money to marry his fiancée.

"Of course it didn't work. Your father put him in his place, but Bennoni got desperate. He went to your house and found you alone. Whatever he said or did, he frightened you pretty badly. When Edward came home he found you hysterical. He sent you back to England immediately.

"He told me everything when he saw us falling in love. He knew he didn't have long to live, and he begged me to protect you from Corrado Bennoni. But after Edward died, Bennoni came to England. He persuaded you that he'd been cheated, and you owed him something. *That* was why you were marrying him. But you came to your senses and tried to run away while there was still time. He doesn't love you, Philippa. All he ever wanted was the money."

"I don't believe it," she said defiantly, but the words sounded hollow to her own ears. This made sense of so much that had puzzled her. Corrado had kept her from contact with the outside world, insisting that she must have space to remember the past for herself. It had seemed like overprotectiveness, but with sudden hideous clarity she saw how it might have hidden something sinister.

If Michael's story was true, it explained why she'd escaped on her wedding day. Had Corrado reasoned that he might use the breathing space of her amnesia to bind her to him with ties of passion that would hold her even when she remembered?

"I don't believe it," she repeated, yet even as she spoke the words the memory of the hobby room in her old home rose up, the sense of terror that had possessed her there and the certainty that it was connected with Corrado. Her father had returned to find her hysterical because of something Corrado had said or done.

"I think you do believe it," Michael said grimly. "Somewhere, deep down under your romantic delusions you *know* he's out for what he can get. Why else do you think he made you sign a settlement giving everything to him."

"No—that was my choice—he's never wanted the money—"

"Doesn't want it? Do you know how often he's been in touch with the firm, laying down the law? He made it impossible for me to call here, but *he's* called *me* time and again demanding to see papers, telling me things had to be done his way."

Philippa's throat went dry as she remembered overhearing one of those calls. "Are *you* the managing director?"

"Yes. Edward appointed me before he died, and I've tried to protect your interests as best I could. But it's been hard when you've given Bennoni so much power. You've fallen into the hands of one of the most cynical, heartless rogues who ever lived. But, thank God, I arrived in time."

She turned away from him, frantically pressing her hands over her ears. But there was no escape from the thoughts he'd insinuated into her mind. The bright dream of love she'd cherished had trembled under a blow from the brutal fist of suspicion. Ugly questions blared inside her head like sirens. Had she flinched from confronting the truth in her old house because deep in her heart she'd known it was too horrible to bear?

"We'll have to hurry," Michael said urgently. "Just come as you are."

"I'm not coming with you. I couldn't—I couldn't do that to him a second time."

"That's his problem," Michael snapped. "Don't waste your pity on him. All the pity he's ever shown you is to manipulate your sickness to his own advantage." He took her shoulders and looked into her face. She wanted to pull away, but there was a snakelike hypnotism in his gaze that paralyzed her. "Listen, darling," he said softly, "the nightmare's over now. I'm here to take you home to safety. You'll get the best medical attention."

"I don't need medical attention," she whispered through the rising tide of pain. "I just need—peace."

Michael's voice became soft and persuasive. "And I'm going to see that you get it. I've already hired nurses who'll look after you night and day until you've recovered from your delusions. You can give me power of attorney so that my lawyers can begin to undo this so-called marriage and recover your property." He began to draw her close, murmuring, "I'm going to care for you so that you never have to worry about anything ever again."

Tears began to roll down her cheeks as she saw how easily it might be true. She was so crazed, so deluded that she had to be watched "night and day" while someone else managed her affairs. She felt Michael's hand tilt her chin up. His lips were cold on hers.

Revulsion spread through her. What was she doing? She tensed herself to push him away, but realized that he, too, had stiffened and drawn back to look at the door.

Corrado stood there, a dreadful look in his eyes.

Philippa jerked out of Michael's arms and stared at Corrado in torment. It was as if she saw two men. The tender, generous lover who'd won her heart and soul stood side by side with the deceitful villain who would stoop to any level to cheat her. She buried her face in her hands.

"I've come to take Philippa home," Michael declared. "Don't try to stop me."

"You?" Corrado gazed at him as though barely recognizing his existence. "You have no business here."

He thrust Michael aside and came over to her, but didn't touch her. "I was afraid of this," he said. "You thought me overcautious, but now you know why. I was trying to protect you from hearing some garbled version of the truth before you remembered it yourself."

"What *is* the truth?" she cried passionately.

"The truth is that he's a liar and a cheat," Michael declared. "And now he's been discovered he thinks he can deceive you again."

Corrado didn't give him so much as a look. "The truth is that your father stole my work," he said to Philippa. "I invented the component that made his fortune. After his death you offered me every penny you possessed in reparation. I could have taken it all without marriage. But I asked you to marry me because I'd fallen in love with you."

"What a sentimental story," Michael said with a sneer. "How noble! But you weren't so noble eight years ago, were you? Don't be fooled, Philippa. Ask him what happened when he went to your home. What was it he did that left you so distraught that your father took you back to England within days?"

She turned anguished eyes on Corrado. "I told you once that I have a cruel temper," he told her. "I was furious and I spoke bitterly to you."

"And Philippa became hysterical just because you lost your temper?" Michael snorted. "Who do you think you're fooling? There must have been a damned sight more than that."

"There was no more than that," Corrado said firmly. "There were...special reasons why she took it hard."

Philippa nodded, not answering. She knew Corrado was subtly reminding her of the infatuation she had for him, but he wouldn't speak of it to Michael. She imagined herself at fifteen, hopelessly in love with him, and she inwardly flinched from the thought of the heartbreak his anger could have caused. Michael's cold voice broke into her thoughts. "Don't believe him. It's a cover-up. He has no proof."

"No, there's no proof," Corrado agreed. "There's only my word, and why should you take that?" He hesitated. "I won't hold you, Philippa. If you want to leave me and marry this man, I'll let you go," he said, as if the words were torn from him.

"Philippa," Michael said urgently, "come with me now."

But she was looking at Corrado. "Do you mean that?" she whispered.

His face was taut with strain and a pulse twitched at the corner of his mouth. "I've done everything I can to convince you of my love. But if I've failed—" he took a harsh breath "—it's better for you to go away than to live with me in doubt. That doubt would eventually destroy us both."

"You'd actually let me go...now?" she repeated incredulously.

His mouth twisted. "I'm not going to keep you prisoner, although I realize you must sometimes have thought I was doing just that."

"Of course you were," Michael said. "When I called, you denied she was here. Then you changed the number to stop me from calling again. What are you but a common kidnapper?"

"Philippa knows what I am," Corrado said. He spoke directly to her. "Whatever I did, I did it to protect you. I couldn't let him get to you with this story. Think what it would have done to you."

"I don't know how I'd have felt," she said softly. "I only know how it hurts to discover that you've been hiding things from me. You shouldn't have done it," she burst out passionately. "You should have told me everything, however bad it seemed. You speak of doubt, but it's *you* who doubted *me*. You should have trusted me with the truth, Corrado."

"You were ill. You couldn't have endured it."

"He wouldn't dare tell you the truth," Michael sneered. "You'd have left him long before this."

She looked at Corrado. "You're saying my father was a common thief. I can't accept that." But she remembered her father's picture, the hard, watchful eyes and her own instinctive feeling that he was untrustworthy.

"Is it easier to believe that *I* am a common thief?" Corrado demanded. "That I've made use of you, that my love has only been a hollow pretense?"

She shook her head, dizzy with strain and anguish. For if that were so, the rest of her life would be empty. She thought of everything they'd shared: his body close to hers, heated with love, his eyes glowing as he looked down at her in his arms, the tenderness and love he'd showered on her. She wanted to scream aloud at the thought that it might all have been no more than a cruel mockery.

"Philippa." Corrado spoke very quietly, but there was a note in his voice she'd never heard before. "How often have you told me that the facts didn't matter? That what counted was the truth you discovered inside yourself, that our love was the only reality?"

It was true. She'd said it many times, and now he was asking her to stand by her words. If her faith wasn't equal to the challenge, then it was she who'd made a mockery of their love.

"You must do whatever you wish," Corrado went on. "Perhaps I've protected you too much, but I always knew this day would come, and I tried to bind you to me with my love. But if the bonds have become chains, it's better to cut them now."

"Come on," Michael urged, taking her arm.

But she pushed him away and turned to Corrado, searching his face as if her life depended on what she found there. "You mean for me to go this minute?" she asked.

"If you intend to leave me, now is the best time," he said, paling at the thought.

"But what about tomorrow...our wedding...?"

"I can take care of the explanations."

"How will you tell them that your bride deserted you for the second time?"

"That's my problem," he said harshly.

She thought of what it would mean to him in this country where male sexual pride counted for so much, the scorn and derision he'd endure as a twice-rejected bridegroom. Yet he'd face it for her sake. It was as though a fog covering her brain had cleared suddenly, revealing a beautiful landscape. She turned slightly and looked at Michael standing by impatiently. Then she took a step closer to Corrado. "You'd better leave, Michael. I'm staying here."

"You're crazy," he snapped. "You can't take his word for anything."

"I can take Corrado's word for the most important thing. When he says he loves me, I believe that. There's nothing else I need to know."

Corrado put an arm about her shoulders, drawing her close to him. "You'd better leave, Radley," he said. "*My wife* has given you your answer."

Defeated, Michael Radley turned to the door, but he stopped for a parting shot. "Don't fool yourself, Bennoni. She's only staying from pity. As for you, Philippa, you're making the biggest mistake of your life. One day you'll remember everything, and then it'll be too late."

"I'm not afraid," she said proudly.

She waited until the door had closed before looking up at Corrado. "Do you pity me?" he demanded harshly.

"I'm staying because I love you," she said urgently, "and you love me. If there's one thing I know, it's that. You'd have let me go, knowing the humiliation you'd have had to face. Nothing less than love would allow you to do that for me."

"But so much that Radley said was true. I *have* kept him away from you. Doesn't that frighten you?"

She shook her head. "I trust you. You said once I'd trust you more if I remembered things of my own accord. I still feel you shouldn't have kept the truth from me all this time, but I can see why you did so at first. Michael was only thinking of himself. He wanted to imprison me with nurses and take control of my life. Thank heavens I saw it in time. When I think you'd have let me go with him..." She shuddered.

"I had to give you the chance. When I came in and saw you in his arms—"

"No," she interrupted fiercely. "You'll never lose me, Corrado. I love you too much to ever leave you."

"I think I didn't know what true love was until you took my word against his," he said huskily. "But if you love me enough to marry me without knowing the truth..."

"But I do know the truth," she said, kissing him tenderly. "The truth is whatever you've told me."

A strange expression came over Corrado's face. For a moment he seemed embarrassed, as though her unquestioning trust had made him ashamed. But it was gone almost at once. He smiled and kissed her, and she told herself she must have been mistaken.

"Will you be all right now?" he asked anxiously. "Shall I stay with you after all?"

"No, I'm fine." She had a desperate need to be alone and to think over what she'd heard.

It was hours before she slept, and then it was the most troubled sleep she'd had since she first awoke after the accident, a stranger to herself. She was tormented by the old nightmare where she faced Corrado's scorn. And once again, just beyond her reach was truth behind his statement that some wrongs could never be made right.

When Philippa threw open the shutters and the dazzling sun streamed into her room, all dark thoughts were banished. Rosa and Senta came to help her with her wedding dress, exclaiming with pleasure as they lifted the beautiful satin and lace garment over her head and settled it about her. The bodice with its modestly high neck fit her slim figure like a second skin before billowing out into full skirts, supported by petticoats.

The veil was attached to a little crown of pearls, which they settled carefully on her head. Philippa looked at the beautiful bride in the mirror, amazed that the traumas of recent weeks had left so little physical trace. All agitation seemed to have passed, leaving only the blissful serenity of a woman who was about to give herself forever to the man she loved.

There was a knock at the door, and Martha told her that Paolo was waiting to take the bride to church. Rosa and Senta escorted her downstairs, and Paolo offered her his arm to the car. Corrado had already gone on ahead.

It was a short journey to the church, and when they arrived a curious little crowd had gathered outside. By now everyone in the village knew the circumstances of this marriage, and Philippa guessed there'd been some speculation about whether she would show up this time at all.

As Paolo helped her out of the car, her eyes moved casually over the spectators, and then she stiffened with shock.

Michael Radley was standing watching her, angry at his loss.

She had to pass close to him. She avoided meeting his eyes, but his presence brought back the warning he'd hurled at her the night before. *One day you'll remember everything and then it'll be too late.*

In the same dreadful moment Aunt Claire's words returned to her: . . . *headstrong and blind to the pitfalls . . . I remember how often you came to grief. . . .*

She walked on into the church, moving automatically. Somewhere above her the organ swelled. She was moving forward on Paolo's arm. She could see Corrado standing by the altar steps. A sense of urgency seized her. She must get to him quickly so that he could silence the voices that tormented her.

She was drawing near enough to see his face, and there was a strange look on it, as though fear had given way to relief so recently that the echo lingered. He, too, had been afraid she wouldn't come. Like her, he could only find peace when they were together.

As they neared the last few steps Paolo released her arm. Suddenly she drew away from him, breaking the rhythm of their measured tread to take a quick step forward, her hand outstretched eagerly to her husband. At the same time he moved toward her, reaching out. Their hands clasped urgently in the space between them.

A rustle went through the congregation at this unorthodox proceeding. But the bride and groom never noticed. The service was no more than a formality now. They'd already claimed each other in the sight of the world.

Don Ferrando smiled, cleared his throat to attract their attention and began the marriage service.

Nine

While the party was in full swing downstairs, Philippa slipped up to her room, followed by Rosa. The bridal couple were to take their honeymoon in the mountains, driving from resort to resort, and it was time for them to leave if they were to make the first stage tonight.

The long mirror reflected the gorgeous dress one last time, and Philippa stopped to survey herself, half expecting to see a change since this morning. She wasn't only a bride. She was a woman who'd embarked on a journey into the unknown.

She remembered a book she'd found on Corrado's shelves. It contained reproductions of old sea maps drawn centuries ago before most of the world was discovered. Outside the tiny area that was known to man someone had written, "Here be dragons." Yet they'd launched their tiny vessels bravely, nonetheless.

She smiled at her own fanciful thoughts, but her heart was high as she changed with Rosa's help. Together with Corrado she was ready to face the dragons.

Corrado had the car waiting by the step, their luggage piled in the back. There was a riot of goodbyes, and then they were pulling away. Philippa waved until the house was out of sight. "We're a bit late setting out," Corrado remarked. "We'll have to hurry if we're to get to the hotel tonight."

The sky ahead of them was streaked with crimson that faded as they drove into a soft, pinkish gray that gradually turned to blue. The air grew fresher as the road climbed, and soon they were surrounded by mountains. When they could see the first faint signs of the moon, Philippa asked, "Do we have much farther to go?"

"Another hour until we get to the hotel."

"But I don't feel like waiting another hour," she said significantly.

"Do you want us to skid off the road?" he growled.

"Well, I certainly want us to *get* off the road as soon as possible. We're just coming to a village. There's bound to be some kind of guest house. You can call the hotel and tell them the car broke down."

A moment later he was pulling up outside a small building with a sign announcing vacant rooms. It looked just about big enough to take two guests at most. They went in and rang the bell, and after a moment the proprietor appeared. He was an old man who seemed surprised at anyone taking the sign seriously, but he showed them up to a room beneath the rafters. Philippa's heart leaped as she saw the huge brass bedstead piled high with pillows.

"You'll be hungry," the proprietor announced. "My wife is a fine cook." He proceeded to elaborate on the choice of food available, while the other two listened, smothering their impatience. Philippa's hand crept to Corrado's, and he enclosed it in a crushing grip. Even through that brief contact his desire communicated itself to her.

At last the old man bustled away, and they dared to meet each other's eyes. "It would have been quicker to go on to the hotel," Philippa said solemnly.

At the same moment they both exploded into laughter. Corrado pulled her against him, and she rocked with mirth until she heard his laughter stop abruptly. Looking up, she saw something in his eyes that made her heart thud. His arms tightened around her, his lips descended to meet hers, and nothing else existed. "Tell me that you love me," he whispered against her mouth.

"Yes—yes—" The words became lost.

He kissed her with irresistible force, enfolding her in an embrace so fierce that she could hardly move her hands as they tried to find him. She was aflame with the need to take him into herself and feel him deep within her. Her passion was rising to danger pitch with electrifying speed, but stronger than passion was the need to reassure herself that he was finally hers at last.

Keeping his mouth on hers, he turned her in his arms and lifted her. She caressed him feverishly, running her hands through his hair, outlining the heavy muscles of his neck. Everything in her was concentrated on Corrado—the feel of his skin, the clean, tangy odor of his body, the hard breadth of his chest against hers. Excitement swirled through her at the thought of the night to come.

She felt the softness against her back as he set her down on the bed and started a swift, determined assault on her clothing. The light material of her dress tore under his fingers. In the past Corrado's lovemaking had always been tempered by tenderness. Now he stripped her with thrilling urgency, and she offered herself willingly. He ripped his own clothes off, tossing them onto the floor, and when they were both naked he lay beside her and took her into his arms.

Warmth swirled through her as he bent his head to claim one nipple with his mouth. She clasped her hands behind his head, feeling the tip of his tongue circle its target softly but with determined intent. When he'd caressed it into a rosy peak he gave his attention to its neighbor. He took his time, teasing her purposefully until she moaned, then burying his face between her ripe breasts, reveling in her.

For a long moment he stayed motionless in blissful content, as though he would absorb her essence into himself through all his senses at once. Then he raised his head to gaze at her with glowing eyes. At that look she reached for him, pressing his body closer to hers, feeling the swell and tautness of muscle beneath the skin. There was steely strength there to set against her softness. But there was strength in her, too, gentler but no less demanding.

She explored him in ways she knew he loved, enjoying the uncontrollable tremors that went through him at the skilled mastery of her fingers. He groaned as she ran her finger down his spine to the swell of his flanks, and she knew he was fighting for control, wanting to take their loving slowly, but finding it more and more difficult with every moment that passed. She began to stroke his lean hips and smooth, flat stomach, lingering there to flex her fingers, watching his face with loving eyes as her caresses became more intimate and provocative.

He returned the provocation with fervor, his hands finding their way to familiar places. The curves and valleys of her body were his. He'd made them his own, and now he reclaimed them, tracing his fingers around, across, behind, between, leaving a trail of fire in their wake, until her whole body was aflame. She murmured his name hazily, reveling in the heat.

"I know what pleases you, Philippa," he growled into her hair, "and for me, there's no greater pleasure."

She wanted him unbearably. She writhed against him, sliding lower so that she could rain kisses over his chest, intoxicated by the hot, musky scent of his arousal. She craved this union with all her being, and her body was aching with frustration.

"I want you, Corrado," she said huskily against his mouth.

"Oh, *cara*, I wanted to hear you say that...."

He moved quickly over her, and in a moment their bodies were united. She quivered ecstatically and arched against him, seeking the fulfillment that was his alone to give.

He made love to her with long, slow thrusts of agonizing sweetness. She was almost demented with the poignancy of those sensations. A moan broke from her, and she curled her legs around him, making him her partner, feeling the tremors shuddering through his muscular frame. His own passion was at danger pitch. She could sense that, even through the iron control that made it possible for him to claim her with such tantalizing slowness. Looking up into his face, she saw his eyes blazing with a light she'd never seen before. There was a fierceness there, but she didn't fear it because it mirrored the primitive storm that was sweeping through herself as well.

The pleasure mounted in intensity as he claimed her with increasing power. She challenged him back, her loins moving in rhythm with his until they reached the peak at the same moment and cried out their release, clinging to each other as the universe swirled darkly about them.

Philippa opened her eyes at last to find the world back in its normal place and her body suffused with a blissful, languorous content. But greater still was the content of her heart. Corrado's chest was beneath her hand, and she could hear the soft thunder from within. She tightened her arms around him and felt his answering embrace.

As summer moved toward its height the heat became almost unbearably intense. Each day the sky presented an unbroken expanse of blue, and the country roads became drier and dustier. It was the time of the harvest, and wherever she went, seeking new subjects for her drawings, Philippa saw the fields swarming with life as the farmers worked to gather their crops.

She felt as though her own life had come to a summer ripening. Surely no marriage had ever been as happy as theirs. And yet . . .

Her thoughts often broke off at this point, and an uneasiness would settle over her. In her heart she knew that Corrado was still concealing something from her. One morning, several weeks after their return from their honeymoon, she awoke to find him sitting by the window in the dawn light, reading what looked like a letter.

She'd held her breath as he folded it deliberately and put it away in a drawer, which he carefully locked. He sat very still for a long time, a thoughtful look on his face. When he came back to bed, Philippa was lying with her eyes closed. She didn't tell him what she'd seen, and he never mentioned it.

She'd always known that his overprotective nature came almost to the point of being overbearing. It might take years of patient love before he was ready to accept that his wife was a strong woman. She loved him as he was. But while she might not blame him, his lack of openness with her made it impossible for her to tell him her own wonderful secret, which she'd only just discovered and longed to share with him.

On the day after she'd seen him with the letter, Philippa went over to Pozzuoli to visit Rosa and sketch the boats. Driving back, she slowed down as she recognized Don Ferrando pedaling laboriously along on a bicycle. She honked her horn to attract his attention, but received no response and was about to pull up alongside him when he swerved suddenly across her path without signaling. She braked sharply, but couldn't avoid him and watched in horror as he vanished in a cloud of dust.

Philippa was terrified. The road was bordered by ditches that were nearly six feet deep. She jumped from the car. There was no sign of the priest, but a stream of splendid Neapolitan curses from the bottom of a ditch told her that he was alive. His head appeared, then he hauled the rest of his considerable bulk up the bank, dragging the bicycle behind him. "Are you hurt?" Philippa asked, obviously worried.

"Not at all," Don Ferrando insisted, vigorously dusting himself off.

"I'm so sorry—"

"Don't be. It was my fault. I was a little preoccupied."

Together they surveyed the bicycle whose front wheel was bent. "I'll give you a ride home," she said. "The bike can go on the roof rack."

She leaned down to help him with it, but he waved her gently aside. "I'm sure I'm as strong as you are," she protested, looking at his white hair.

"Yes, perhaps, but I'd rather not have you straining yourself now," he said, giving her a searching look, which made her feel self-conscious. He threw the bike up and lashed it to the rack, then squeezed into the passenger seat, fanning himself madly.

"Why are you riding a bike anyway?" Philippa asked as she started the engine. "Don't tell me your car's being repaired *again*?" A resigned groan was the only answer. "Don't you think it's time you had a new car, Don Ferrando?"

The old man grinned. "You won't believe this, but that car is only three years old."

She did believe it. If Don Ferrando drove a car with the same attention he gave to riding a bicycle, the car's condition was fully accounted for. But tactfully she limited herself to the observation, "It looks a hundred."

"Yes but..." His voice became aggrieved, "I always seem to be the innocent victim of circumstance. Every chicken in the district tries to commit suicide under my wheels, and when I swerve I always hit something. Last time it was the town hall. And the devil himself makes the roads change direction when they see me coming. Mind you," he added grudgingly, "perhaps I do go just a tiny bit too fast—" He heard Philippa's chuckle and went on, "All right, all right, I go a *lot* too fast. But I'm always unlucky."

"I think you were very lucky this time. You could have broken a leg in a fall like that."

"Well, at least it was dry. It's worse if you fall into a ditch in winter," he informed her with the authority of experience. "There's nothing as bad as a ditch full of cold water."

Yes, Philippa thought, cold muddy water. And suddenly she saw the hood of a car nose-diving down the bank at night. She heard the thud as it came to a halt, then total silence except for the drumming in her head. She watched herself struggling out, felt the chill of falling into the shallow water...then nothing, as though a film had run out.

Her hand gripped the wheel in a sudden convulsive movement as she realized that she'd remembered something. For the first time since that night a tiny corner of the dark curtain that hid her past had been lifted.

"Of course, it wouldn't have happened if I'd had my mind on the road," Don Ferrando was saying, "but I'd been trying to decide what text I was going to use for the harvest service."

"Oh yes...the harvest," Philippa echoed automatically.

"But I might as well spare myself the effort," he rumbled on. "Because there's really only one text for the harvest, and my flock would never forgive me if I didn't use it." He began to recite: "'To everything there is a season, and a time to every purpose under heaven: a time to be born, and a time to die; a time to plant, and a time to pluck up that which is planted.' Beautiful words, and I imagine some of them at least sound especially beautiful to you just now."

"Rosa said something like that," she murmured. "She said the time had to be right."

"Rosa's a wise woman, but I meant something slightly different," Don Ferrando said gently.

Philippa came out of her haze to discover that she'd drawn up outside his house with no recollection of how she'd gotten there. The old priest was smiling at her. Philippa smiled back as she caught his meaning. "Yes, they are beautiful words," she said.

He insisted on getting the bike down without her help. Philippa refused his offer to come inside for a coffee. She wanted to be alone to think. "Be careful how you drive on the way home, Philippa—and take good care of yourself," he called in farewell.

As she covered the short distance home she repeated to herself, "A time to be born..." The old man who'd baptized a thousand children had spotted her condition at once. Anna too had probably guessed. Only Corrado didn't know. Something was holding her back.

To everything there is a season....

What had happened this afternoon was the clearest possible sign that she was ready to confront her past. Once she'd almost remembered as she'd stood in her old home and felt the dread of an undiscovered secret that seemed to threaten her. But she'd backed away.

Rosa had as good as told her that she could remember if she truly wanted to. Now those words came back to her like a challenge.

She'd reached her own gate. She could see the house and Anna leaning from a window. She stopped in the act of turning in and sat, tense with indecision. Then she moved resolutely toward the gears, thrust the car into reverse, pulled sharply away and back onto the road. A moment later she was heading in the direction of Naples.

It took half an hour to reach the outskirts of the city. She located the road and drove slowly along it looking for the beaten track that led to her old home. At last she found it. Her heart was beating with apprehension as she saw the house come into view. She drew up in front of the door, left the car and stood gazing at the building, trying to force herself to take the next step. The shuttered windows looked more forbidding than ever, as if warning her that she entered at her own peril.

At last she forced herself to go around the side of the house to the place where they'd entered last time. She had a moment of ridiculous hope that someone would have nailed up the door, but it stood slightly ajar, just as they'd left it. She paused outside, took a deep breath and pushed it inward.

Perhaps because she was alone the gloom struck her more forcibly than last time. The silence, broken only by the sound of her own footsteps, was unnerving. Philippa walked through the rooms, pausing here and there, trying vainly to conjure up memories. But in her heart she knew she was only trying to postpone the inevitable moment when she'd have to go to the hobby room and discover whatever awaited her there.

At last she pushed open the door and stepped tentatively inside. The shutters were closed, but a few bars of sunlight seeped through the cracks, giving enough light for her to find where she'd been standing last time. She didn't open the shutters as she had before, but stood there in the semidarkness, silently invoking her ghosts.

After a while she felt the fear begin to press in on her. She took a firmer stance, refusing to listen to the inner voice that urged her to escape. Her heart was pounding, and the air about her was like a suffocating blanket. She was trapped inside it, trying to fight her way out, knowing that the truth was just a little way off if only she had the courage to stand her ground. She was cold with shock and trembling violently, but she stayed where she was.

Then suddenly it was over. Everything was still and quiet about her. The curtains that had shrouded her mind fell apart, revealing the backward path of her life.

She knew the truth. She knew what Corrado had tried so hard to protect her from discovering too soon. And she knew why.

"No!" she screamed. *"I don't believe it. It can't be true. It can't be true!"*

Ten

She could see that other Philippa very clearly now, a bright-faced fifteen-year-old with the awkward elegance of a colt, on the verge of blooming into beautiful womanhood. Dressed in jeans, an old shirt and sandals, she was running through the winding streets of Naples toward the quay, her heart beating with eagerness because she was going to see the young man she adored.

She knew Corrado saw her only as the kid sister he'd never had. He thought of nothing but Maria now. He'd even taken Philippa sailing and told her it would be for the last time. She'd landed on a small island and flirted with him naively, trying to make him see her as a woman, but he hadn't seemed to understand.

But this particular evening Maria was away, and she'd found an excuse to visit the little house by the water where he lived with his parents.

Details came fast as the memories of that day flooded back to her. Rosa was there in the kitchen. She smiled kindly and said, "He's in the shed."

She went out into the yard to find the battered old shed that Corrado used as a workshop. He was inside, hunched over a small table, working on a drawing that was absorbing all his attention. Other drawings lay scattered around him as though he'd had second and third thoughts. As Philippa watched he crushed another paper, tossed it aside and started again on a plain sheet.

At first he didn't notice her, and the young girl stood watching him, aching with hopeless love. He was twenty-four, a lean, long-limbed young god with skin bronzed by the sun and the brilliant light that was reflected from the sea. He had dark, eloquent eyes that made her heart turn over when he smiled at her.

He looked up and grinned, saying "Ciao *piccina*." She scowled. She hated to be called *piccina*, which meant "little one." He'd first said it when she was ten, on the day he'd started work for her father, and now it made her feel that he still saw her as ten years old.

"Ciao," she responded, trying to sound nonchalant so that he wouldn't guess her heart was beating madly. "I just came to bring you a message from my father. He's worried about those new plugs. Can you see to them first thing tomorrow?"

"Sure." He smiled, too kind to show that he'd seen through the transparent excuse. "Are you staying for supper?"

She shrugged elaborately. "I don't know. I'm awfully busy."

"My mother will be hurt if you don't stay."

"In that case... to please your mother."

He returned to his drawing. She wanted desperately for him to talk to her. But she was afraid to be a nuisance in case he sent her away. So she made a pretense of looking around his workshop, studying the titles of the books on the shelves. They were mostly about design and electronics, but there was also a volume of Dante's poetry. As she had an essay about Dante to write for school, she pulled out the volume and settled down to read.

She found it difficult to concentrate because of the temptation to look up and study his dark head, bent over his work. He seemed oblivious to her, and she could watch him with bittersweet happiness.

Once he glanced up. Philippa blushed to be caught staring and mumbled, "Do you have something to write with, so that I can make notes for my essay?"

He handed her a pencil and returned to his work. She snatched up one of his discarded sheets and made a great play of taking notes. But she needn't have bothered. He'd forgotten her at once.

She didn't know what they ate for supper. She was devouring Corrado with her eyes, storing up every detail of his image. He seemed abstracted, and occasionally he smiled to himself. After supper he said, "Come on, *piccina*. I'll run you home."

When they were on the road, Philippa said, "You were very quiet over supper tonight. Is anything wrong?"

"Wrong? Far from it. I'm in a mood to celebrate. Very soon I'll be setting my wedding day."

Her heart lurched painfully. "But—you said—it wouldn't be for a long time—"

"But that was before—" He checked himself.

"Before?" she echoed.

He shook his head. "No, I promised myself I wouldn't say anything until I was certain, not even to you, *piccina*."

"I can keep a secret," she pleaded.

"I know you can. But it's bad luck to speak too soon." He added half to himself, "And yet I've done it, I know I have. Nothing can go wrong now." He gave her hand a squeeze in their old, comradely way. "You'll be the first person after Maria to know everything, I promise. But for tonight...just be happy for me."

"Of course," she said bravely.

It was dark when he pulled up outside her home and said cheerfully, "Good night. Sweet dreams."

The casual brotherliness in his tone hurt almost as much as knowing that she would soon lose him altogether. Her throat was aching with unshed tears. She tried to bid him good-night but couldn't get the words out, and suddenly she gave way to the anguished intensity of her young love, flinging her arms about his neck and kissing him on the mouth.

He stiffened with surprise and began to push her away. But then he stopped and held her gently, neither responding nor rejecting. She drew back and looked up into his eyes, but instead of what she'd hoped to find there was only kindness and understanding. "You're becoming a woman," he said gently.

"I *am* a woman, and . . . and I love you." She saw him shake his head and said urgently, "I do. I love you more than Maria ever will."

"Philippa, listen to me. You don't love me. What do you know of love at fifteen? One day you'll love a man with all your heart, and then you'll look back on that fellow you once knew in Naples and wonder what you ever saw in him."

"No," she said, tears choking her voice.

He took her face between his hands and said, "You're going to be so beautiful. Don't be in a rush to find love. It'll find you soon enough." He stopped and drew in his breath suddenly, as though he'd seen something that took him aback, then he dropped his head and laid his lips tenderly on hers.

For a long moment she lay in his arms while the stars whirled about her. She'd dreamed of his kiss, but it was more sweet than she'd ever dared to hope. She could smell the wind and the sea on his skin, and the enticing aroma made her heart beat with the stirring of desire. She felt his arms tighten about her, as though his control had slipped, and his lips began to move dangerously over her own. His mouth was warm and persuasive, enticing her to the brink of wonderful discoveries. Unconsciously she let her lips fall apart, and a sigh of happiness escaped her.

Abruptly Corrado stiffened, and a tremor went through him. He pulled his mouth from hers and said unsteadily, "What am I doing? You're a child... but God forgive me, for a moment I nearly forgot." He drew a ragged breath. "*Piccina*, the man who loves you and wins your love in return will be very lucky. In another life...I think it would have been me. Now go, quickly."

She broke away and jumped out of the car. He drove off at once, and she was alone with the warm night and the stars, with her bliss and heartache.

Later, as she was getting ready for bed, a paper dropped out of her jeans. It was the one she'd taken from Corrado's workshop, pretending to make notes. She put it on her bedside table.

As she was snuggling under the sheet there was a knock on her door, and her father came in. "Good night, pet," he said, crossing to the bed. As he leaned down to kiss her, his eyes fell on the paper. "What's this?" he asked, turning it over to the drawing.

"It's something Corrado was doing. He's always making little sketches."

Her father grunted in reply. She bid him a hasty good-night, anxious to be alone so that she could relive her memories of Corrado's kiss. She didn't even notice that the paper had disappeared with him.

She lay awake that night thinking of Corrado, never dreaming that she'd set in motion a train of events that was to change the course of so many lives and devastate her own.

The next few weeks she held her breath waiting to hear about Corrado's marriage, but the blow didn't fall. She saw little of her father, but when she did see him he had that same air of suppressed excitement that she'd seen in Corrado. Then one day he came in beaming and said, "How would you like to go back to England, pet?"

"You mean for good?"

"That's right. Things are changing for us. We'll have a beautiful house in London and another one in the country and a horse for you and—"

"Daddy, what's happened?"

"What's happened is the 'Davison plug.' It's going to put me right on top of the electronics pile. I've just signed the first deal, and we're going to be rich." He kissed her exuberantly. "Rich, darling, *rich*!"

The next day while she was working in her hobby room, she heard Corrado fling open the front door and call her name. She jumped up eagerly to greet him. But when he came bursting into her room the greeting died on her lips.

Corrado was deathly pale, his eyes were wild, and he was visibly shaking. Her first thought was that he must be ill, but then she saw the look he turned on her and instinctively took a step back. He was in a murderous rage. "You deceitful, cunning little spy," he spat at her. "You sly, two-faced traitor. To think I was fond of you. My parents welcomed you to their home, and you repay us like this."

"Corrado, please, I don't—"

She was silenced by a blast of cold hate that left her reeling. She'd never seen Corrado's temper, never realized he was capable of such cruel, razor-sharp words. "Your father's going to make a fortune on what he stole from me," he raged. "They call him a genius because he invented the 'Davison plug.' But it was *my* invention. He stole it from one of my drawings that you gave him."

"You mean—"

"I mean the paper you took from my workshop. I numbered all my rough drafts, and I knew one was missing after you were there. I thought I'd lost it, until I found my invention had been patented by your father in his own name."

"Oh, dear God," she whispered. "I didn't mean to—it was an accident, Corrado. You can't believe I did it on purpose."

"What does it matter why you did it?" he shouted. "Do you think it makes a difference whether you acted out of spite or stupidity? I was going to get married on the strength of that work."

If he'd struck her it would have been easier to endure than the hate and scorn she saw in his eyes. But he kept his distance, lashing her with cruel, contemptuous words, until she was trembling violently. "There's been a mistake," she tried to say through her tears. "My father didn't understand—I'll talk to him—"

"Your father knew perfectly well what he was doing," he stormed. "*Talk* to him? I tried that today and got thrown out of the factory. I've been threatened with arrest if I 'make any more trouble.' Now do you realize what you've done?"

Her desperate plea for his forgiveness only produced a grim laugh. "Forgive you? I'd as soon kiss a snake. There are some wrongs that can never be made right. Remember that," he said with a sneer.

He walked out without a backward glance. She ran after him, crying out his name, trying to hold onto him, but he shrugged her off and got into his old car. She watched it disappear before running back into the house and throwing herself onto the sofa to sob out her despair. She lay there shivering until her father came home and found her.

It never occurred to her to question Corrado's word. Even at fifteen she knew her father wasn't a scrupulous man, and she disbelieved his denials. She was sick at what she'd innocently done and longed for a chance to see Corrado and once more beg his forgiveness. But Edward hurried her back to England, and Corrado disappeared from her life.

The Davison plug made Edward a millionaire, then a multimillionaire. For eight years Philippa lived the life of a woman who had everything. Edward lavished anything money could buy on her, but father and daughter looked at each other across a widening abyss. He was trying to wipe the look of reproach from her eyes, and she was trying to forget Corrado's same look, which had haunted her since she was fifteen. They both failed.

Edward began to groom Michael Radley as his successor. He would have liked to have seen his daughter married to Michael and managed to nudge her into a halfhearted engagement, but Philippa resisted all attempts to make her set the date.

Then Edward became seriously ill, and within three months he was dead. Philippa stood by his grave, barely hearing the priest reading the final words of the burial service, and blamed herself for not loving him more. But her love had died when he'd used her to destroy Corrado Bennoni.

Suddenly her eyes fell on one man standing slightly apart from the crowd, and she stiffened with shock. Her lips almost shaped the name she hadn't uttered for eight years.

He was older, not just with the passage of years, but because he looked as if all the joy had been driven from his life long ago. He stood motionless except for his hair that was ruffled by the winter breeze, and his gaze never once left Philippa's.

"Thou knowest, Lord, the secrets of our hearts..." The prayer was coming to an end. Michael took hold of her arm and tried to draw her away to the waiting car, but she detached herself firmly and walked over to Corrado. "Ciao," she said.

After a moment's surprise he replied, "Ciao."

She went on, still in Italian, "I hadn't expected to see you...here," she said quietly, checking the impulse to say "ever again."

"I read about your father's death in the papers. I'm sorry, Philippa. It must have been difficult for you."

"He faded away so quickly at the end. He'd always seemed strong before."

"I remember." He looked uneasy.

"Where are you staying?" she asked, desperate not to let the silence fall.

"At the Alton Hotel."

"Darling, we ought to be going now." Michael had appeared at her side, taking her elbow in an insistent movement. He nodded coldly to Corrado.

She had to endure the reception in Edward's palatial mansion, and it was many hours before it was over and she could drop onto the sofa. "I suppose that was Corrado Bennoni?" Michael said, sitting beside her. "I guessed when I heard you speaking Italian."

"Yes," she said, staring at the ceiling.

"To think of him having the nerve to turn up here."

"Yes, to think of him turning up here," she echoed abstractedly. "Michael, did it ever strike you as strange that my father never invented anything else after the Davison plug?"

"No, it didn't," he answered firmly. "Edward wouldn't be the only man to have just one stroke of inspiration. Look, I know what's happened. Seeing Bennoni has unsettled you, but you can't believe anything he says. Edward told me all about it. Bennoni did a few sketches to Edward's specifications, that's all. He hasn't a shadow of a claim."

"That's what my father told you?"

"Yes, I guess he saw this happening. But don't worry. I promised I'd protect you."

Philippa turned her head and looked at him curiously. "Protect me—or yourself?"

"I don't know what you're talking about."

"Our marriage," she said lightly. "Let's face it, if I got an attack of conscience about how much of my inheritance really belongs to Corrado it would, shall we say, take the gilt off the wedding cake?"

He flushed angrily. "I think that remark's in the worst possible taste."

"You mean, you'd take me 'for poorer' just as readily as 'for richer'?"

"Philippa, have you been drinking?"

"No, but it's strange how light-headed I feel," she mused.

"Well, that's hardly surprising, considering the strain you've been under," he conceded. "I'll leave you now, and I want you to go straight to bed as soon as I've gone."

He drew her toward him and kissed her with exceptional ardor, almost as if he were trying to silence her suspicions, she thought wryly. At last he drew back, frowning at her lack of responsiveness. "I'm really very tired," she said apologetically.

After he'd left, Philippa stayed where she was, staring into space, motionless except for the nervous drumming of her fingers. Then she sat up with an abrupt, decisive movement, pulled the phone toward her and called the Alton Hotel.

They studied each other quietly, like two cats circling.

"You've changed," Philippa said at last. She knew the words were inadequate to describe the subtle alteration that had more to do with experience than years. There was a new hardness in his eyes, and the hint of austerity in his face was more marked.

It was there in his voice, too, when he answered coolly, "That was to be expected. You've changed far more. What became of that tousled girl in jeans?"

"She died a long time ago," Philippa said lightly. "Do you mind if I sit down?"

"By all means. Where were my manners?"

His formal politeness dismayed her. At the graveside she'd seen an intensity in his eyes that suggested he was mastering strong emotions. But now, in the anonymous surroundings of his hotel room, all emotion was stripped from his manner, and he spoke as coolly as any stranger.

But then, what had she expected? He had no reason to think kindly of her. He hadn't spent eight years haunted by their last meeting. Seeing him again, Philippa realized that she'd always believed they would one day meet again and somehow set matters right. But this Corrado was a different person from the warmhearted, laughing young man she'd known. He was a stern-faced stranger, armored in chilly, defensive courtesy, and she didn't know how to talk to him.

As she moved to a chair he stepped close to help her remove her mink coat, and she was suddenly burningly aware of its outrageous luxury. Corrado's room was lovely, but it was far below what he could have commanded if he hadn't been robbed. It was Philippa, the innocent thief, who wore the fruits of his work on her back, and who'd stupidly come here flaunting them. Sackcloth and ashes would have been more appropriate, she thought bitterly, and her cheeks flushed with shame.

"Can I get you a drink?" he asked politely.

"Yes, please." She didn't want a drink, but it would help cover the gap that yawned between them. Everything had seemed so easy on her way here, but now all the things she'd planned to say had deserted her.

"Are you here alone?" she asked finally. "I thought you might have brought your wife."

"I have no wife. I've been too busy to marry."

She'd thought she was on her guard, but there was no defense against the stab of pleasure his words gave her. "You lost Maria then? I'm sorry."

"Don't be. It wouldn't have worked. A man travels faster and farther alone."

"And have you traveled very far?"

"Not as far as I intend to go. I have a couple of factories. I got the first by buying up a place that was going bankrupt. I couldn't offer very good terms, but the other side wasn't in a position to be choosy. I made it a going concern and in the process learned a lot about how to survive in business.

"I bought the second under the noses of several other people who'd have liked to get hold of it. It's expanded to its limit, and pretty soon I'll be ready to take over some of my rivals. Some of them won't like that, but they won't be able to stop me. Electronics is a cutthroat business, and I've discovered, with some pleasure, that I can cut throats with the best of them."

"Yes," she said wryly. "You learned from masters, didn't you?"

"I wasn't referring to that. It's a waste of time to brood over things irrevocably in the past. I fight back, which is more profitable in every way. Why do you look like that?" he asked as she sighed softly.

"Oh, nothing. It's just that it seems so odd to hear you talking about profit as if that were all there was to life."

"To some lives," he put in quietly.

"I can remember when you said if a man had a happy family, good friends and a bottle of wine, he had all he needed. Even when . . . when you invented the plug, your first thought was that you'd have enough to marry on."

"Good Lord. What a memory you have. I'm sure I've said a great many extremely foolish things in my life."

He sounded merely amused, and she wondered desperately if there was any way to find a handle on the smooth surface he presented. Her stomach was churning with nerves, and it took all her courage to reach out to him, but he deflected her every time. "Corrado," she said impulsively, "I'm sorry for what happened. I know it's inadequate, but I must say it. I acted innocently. Tell me you believe that."

He shrugged. "Of course I believe it. Besides, you wrote to me apologizing, don't you remember?"

"But you never answered."

"As a matter of fact I did answer, but you know your father's methods."

"Yes, of course," she said blankly. "I suppose he must have taken your letter."

"Well, it's water under the bridge now. I told you, it's fatal to brood about past wrongs. Learn from them, then let them go."

She didn't need to ask what he'd learned. It was there in the cool indifference with which he contemplated her. Time and bitter experience had made Corrado coldly ambitious, and the woman trying painfully to atone for old injuries was merely an irrelevance. She could have wept, but pride made her answer him evenly. "What did you say in your letter?"

"I believe I asked your forgiveness for the things I said to you at our last meeting. It was wrong of me to be so angry. It wasn't your fault."

"Then you haven't been hating me all these years?"

"I thought I'd made that plain."

There was a finality in his tone that made it impossible to continue, but she was left feeling that nothing was changed.

"Why did you come here?" Corrado demanded abruptly.

Philippa shrugged as casually as she could. "I want to talk business."

"Is this how you usually do it?"

"If it's the only way I can get to see someone. I could hardly have asked you to come to the head office of Davison Enterprises."

"No, I imagine the guard dogs have been alerted to keep me out."

She laughed brittlely. "You don't know how right you are. Michael's determined to 'protect' me from you."

"I assume Michael is the blond Englishman who made such a point of calling you darling."

"Yes."

"But you reject his protection?"

"Why should I be afraid when I've come here to offer you everything?"

He stared at her, his face unreadable. "And what exactly does 'everything' consist of?" he asked at last.

"Twenty million pounds... give or take the odd penny. The past isn't over, Corrado. It'll never be over while I'm living on stolen money. I've come to give it back."

Eleven

"You always did have a sense of the dramatic. I see it hasn't deserted you," Corrado said with a laugh.

"This is no joke," Philippa said sharply, stung by the indulgent dismissal in his voice. "I'm only restoring what's rightfully yours."

He raised an eyebrow, giving his face a satirical look. "You give money away very coolly, Philippa. I wonder what you'd say if I accepted that wild offer."

"I *want* you to accept it."

"I'm sure you do, for the moment. But I know what you're like. You always did mad things on the spur of the moment and counted the cost later. Often the cost was quite a shock. I remember when you saw a shoal of fishes beneath the boat and dived in because you wanted to catch one with your hands. Of course the water was deeper than you'd thought, I had to go in after you, and we nearly drowned together."

"Yes, I remember that," she said, laughing shakily.

"And here you are, ready to dive into deep water again. Who'd pull you out this time? Your Englishman?"

She thought of Michael, who often lectured her about her reckless ways and of Corrado, who'd never lectured but simply pulled her out of trouble, time and again, by the scruff of her neck. Looking up she saw her memories reflected in his eyes, and a flash of the old camaraderie passed between them. But it vanished at once. "I won't need pulling out this time," she said. "I've made up my mind, and my decision's final."

"I might have something to say about that. You certainly can't force me to take it."

"But it's simple justice. Why should you refuse?" She was hurt and disappointed. Corrado wasn't reacting as he should. He was merely patronizing, as if she were only a rich doll amusing herself by playing with ideas.

"I haven't said I refuse," he replied slowly. "I need time to think. It may be justice, but it's far from simple. I suggest we talk about it tomorrow after we've both had a good night's sleep."

"That's an excellent idea," Philippa said quickly. "I'll be here at eleven." She rose and prepared to leave. At once Corrado was at her side with the coat, punctiliously courteous as he draped it around her shoulders, not letting his hands linger for a moment more than necessary. Even so, his light touch unnerved her.

What nonsense! she thought. I'm not fifteen anymore.

She bade him good-night and left quickly, her heart unaccountably light at the thought of tomorrow.

She lay awake for an hour that night, then got up and made herself some tea. Sooner or later she was going to have to admit the cause for her inner disturbance. Corrado threatened her peace in ways that had nothing to do with the wrong she'd done him. When she'd seen him at the cemetery the rest of the world had seemed to vanish, and she'd known that she'd been waiting for this moment for eight lonely years.

She wondered if it was the same with him, but there'd been no joy in his voice when she'd called him, only a wariness that she'd seen reflected in his eyes when he opened his door to her. He wasn't sitting up, wakeful in the darkness, thinking of her, and that certainty spread a sad ache over heart.

She arrived the next day in her sleek white sports car and found him waiting outside. As soon as she opened the door he got into the passenger seat and said, "Drive on, quickly."

Mystified by his tone Philippa pulled out immediately. Corrado had twisted around so that he could look out of the back window. She glanced at her rearview mirror and saw a black car, which had been parked opposite the hotel, pull out and begin to follow. "I'm sure he was there when I left yesterday evening," she said.

"He's been there all night," Corrado agreed. "I wondered if I was imagining things, but he's following us very closely."

"You mean we're being *spied* on?" she demanded in outrage.

"You said your Englishman was determined to protect you. Look, I don't want to cause you any trouble. I told you to drive on because I wanted to make sure. But now I have, perhaps we should go back."

"The hell with that," she said shortly, and put her foot on the gas. The car shot forward. In the mirror she could see the other car immediately pick up speed. Indignation held her speechless for a moment before she exploded, "I'll have Michael's head for this!"

"Is that his ring you're wearing?"

"What if it is? It doesn't give him the right to set spies on me."

"It doesn't augur well for your marriage," Corrado agreed. "By the way, what are those books on the back seat?"

"Some of the records of Davison Enterprises. I collected them on my way here." She turned quickly into a side street, then took another, turning almost at once, but a glance in the mirror showed the black car still on her tail.

The next few minutes were exciting, and when they were over Corrado released his breath. "You're a very imaginative driver," he said, choosing his words carefully.

"I terrify Michael," she laughed. "He's always trying to persuade me to sell this and buy something more sedate."

"But you take no notice? You're quite right. He'll get enough of his own way when you're married."

He seemed unconscious of having made a provocative statement, and Philippa let it pass. Her attention was given to shaking off her tail, and soon she had her chance. A set of traffic lights appeared ahead of them. She crossed just before they changed to red and saw the other car come to an abrupt halt. "He didn't dare jump the lights," she said delightedly. "There's a policeman watching. Now's our chance."

Corrado kept his eyes fixed on the rearview mirror. "There's no sign of him," he said a few minutes later. "You must have shaken him off."

"Good."

"But where do we go from here?"

"Wait and see."

In half an hour they'd left the city and were driving through country roads. Bare trees lined their way, and the sky was gray and forbidding. Here and there patches of snow could still be seen, growing more pronounced as they went deeper into the countryside.

At last Philippa turned into a dirt road and in a moment had pulled up beside a cottage. "This is it," she said, jumping out. "I found it last year. It was in terrible shape, but I bought it and renovated it."

She shivered as she got out of the car and hurried to the door, fumbling with the keys in her eagerness to get inside. "Why are you wearing that cloth coat?"

Corrado demanded. "The fur you wore yesterday is much more suited for this weather."

"Oh, I don't know," she said vaguely. "I thought I'd give this one an outing."

He sighed. "You're being absurd, Philippa. You don't have to atone by catching pneumonia." For the first time he sounded like his old self, and she was thrilled that he'd understood her so easily.

Inside, the cottage was a skillful combination of the apparently rustic and the actually modern. She shut the doors on the freezing world outside, turned on the heating and hurried into the kitchen. "I'll make us some coffee," she called.

He came and stood watching her. "When your fiancé learns that his spies have lost the scent, will he chase you to this place?" he asked.

"Michael doesn't know about it."

He raised an eyebrow. "You've never brought him here to be alone together?"

"It's a place of work, not a love nest."

"But it's perfect for a love nest. Surely it could do double duty?"

"Well, it doesn't," she said shortly.

She concentrated on what she was doing, aware that Corrado's dark, unsmiling eyes were on her. When she'd handed him his coffee she watched anxiously as he sipped it. To her relief he nodded. "You still make coffee like an Italian," he said approvingly.

"That's your mother's teaching."

"I'll tell her. She'll be delighted."

"How are your parents?"

"My father died a few years ago, so my mother went back to Pozzuoli to live with my Aunt Senta." He talked about his mother for a while. To her relief he seemed easier in her company this morning, as if their escape had broken down some of the barriers.

He began to move around the cottage, which consisted of one large room and kitchen downstairs and one bedroom and bathroom upstairs. "It's my retreat," she told him. "I use it to come here and draw."

Corrado took up some of the pen-and-ink drawings that lay scattered about and studied them with a draftsman's eye. "They're excellent," he commented, "well constructed and full of atmosphere. What do you do with them when they're finished?"

"I sell them," she said, stung by the implication that she was only dallying. "They sell very well."

He laughed. "I'm sure they do. It just didn't occur to me. I don't suppose you need to earn your living."

"That's very true," she agreed with a touch of self-derision. "For eight years I've had a comfortable life on the fruits of your invention." She gave a rhetorical flourish. "Edward Davison's spoiled daughter, who never lacked anything...except the thing she really wanted."

"And what was that?"

"Your forgiveness," she said quietly.

He shrugged. "You have it. I told you, the past is over. I bear you no ill will."

But she couldn't take any comfort from this. It was too easy, and the statement obviously meant nothing to him. "But I bear myself ill will. I've never been happy living on your money, and now I won't have to."

"Your offer's still open then? I thought you'd have come to your senses by now."

"My offer will remain open until you come to your senses and accept it."

"I wish I could convince you that there's no need for you to feel any guilt."

"I took everything away from you—"

"You took nothing away from me," he interrupted. "I was upset at the time, but I've since understood that I owe you a great deal. If I'd become a rich man at twenty-four it would have been the end of me. With nothing to spur me on I'd have grown idle. By now I'd have a paunch and a mind pickled in aspic. Instead I've had to fight, and although it's been a hard struggle I've enjoyed it. My big triumphs are in the future instead of the past. So you see, I have a lot to thank you for."

"Except that you're alone."

"What a romantic you are. I haven't spent the last eight years alone, I promise you." His smile was filled with sensual memory, and her heart lurched painfully. "My life has been far more interesting than if I'd married," he assured her. "Perhaps I should thank you for that, too."

"I'd prefer you didn't," she said shortly. The pain in her heart was overwhelming despite the fact that she knew he certainly hadn't been waiting for her all these years. He was a man in his prime. That was plainly written in the lines of his face, in his taut, muscular body and lithe movements.

The Corrado she'd once loved had been a handsome lad with boyish features and a laugh that was a full-hearted surrender to joy. When he smiled it never reached his eyes now—they remained tense and wary with all traces of boyishness gone.

He was less handsome but more attractive. He had stern, even harsh features, as though he'd been through the fire and survived by discovering his own ruthlessness. He was dangerous in a way he'd never been before, and in that danger lay a challenge. Philippa was sure many women must have found him desirable.

She remembered the kiss he'd given her years before, the surprise on his face. She'd carried his words in her heart for eight years: *The man who loves you and wins your love will be very lucky. In another life I think it would have been me.*

The passage of time had created another life, but it was obvious he didn't love her. When he'd let go of his hate he'd forgotten her. But she would never forget. That realization hit Philippa with frightening clarity. Her heart had remained frozen all these years, waiting for him to return and warm it again. The pain she could feel was the reawakening of her love as the ice melted.

Looking into the eyes of this stranger she saw only cynicism and a refusal to admit his wounds. He was invulnerable to her because he'd chosen to be. She took a slow breath to steady herself against a feeling of desolation. "I think we should start going through the books," she said firmly.

He shrugged. "If you insist."

Philippa spread the books out on the table, and he came over to sit beside her. She began to explain the accounts, trying to keep her tone businesslike, but Corrado was sitting only a few inches away, and she found herself strangely affected by an aura that seemed to radiate from him. The atmosphere of sun and breeze and sea, which had once seemed a part of him, had given way to something less definable, created more by his own power and self-confidence.

As the cottage grew warmer he'd thrown off his jacket and pulled open the collar of his shirt. She could clearly see how he'd filled out in the past years. He'd always had a wiry, nervous strength, tempered by gentleness. Now his well-muscled arms could easily persuade a woman to forget everything else in the world.

"Are you going to daydream all day?" Corrado sounded slightly annoyed. "I've asked you twice what this column of figures means."

"I'm sorry." She came back to the present with a start and forced herself to concentrate as she continued her explanations. Despite his protestations of indifference she could see Corrado was becoming interested, and he asked many searching questions.

"You seem to know all about it," he commented at last. "Have you been involved in the firm?"

"No, but Dad liked me to know what was going on," she replied vaguely. She couldn't tell Corrado how her father had been eager to teach her, and how every lesson had resolved into a boast of how well he'd done for Philippa and how lucky she was. She knew that Edward was implicitly pleading for her approval, and his failure to win it had always hurt him.

It was late afternoon and the light had faded, but Corrado continued to pore over the books. Philippa tidied up the cottage and prepared a light snack. He'd settled down at the table and glanced briefly up to thank her abstractedly.

There'd been no passion and little warmth in his eyes. But it soothed her that he was here. Despite his coolness toward her, his hold on her heart was still as powerful as it had been eight years ago.

Finally he leaned back in his chair, stretching and yawning. As they sat over black coffee, Philippa asked anxiously, "Well?"

"Tell me, Philippa, what do you think of the state of the firm?"

"I think it's beginning to stagnate," she said after thinking for a moment. "Basically it's a one-product firm. Dad diversified into other things, but what made the real money was always your plug. Now it needs someone to give it a push in a new direction."

"Yes, I'd say it's not performing to capacity. Your shareholders seem to have been pretty complacent."

"They didn't have much choice. Dad always kept control by owning the majority of the shares. And, of course, they trusted him because they thought of him as the design genius who made it all happen."

She spoke ironically, but Corrado didn't seem to notice. "I see Michael Radley's been on the board for four years, and your father's deputy for the last two."

"Father was grooming him for the succession. He said he was a sound man."

"But has he planned for the day something supersedes the plug?"

"I don't think it's ever occurred to him," Philippa said. "That's why you've got to take control of the company, Corrado."

"It's heartbreaking to think how it could go downhill if I don't. But then, what happens to you?"

"Don't worry about me."

"I must. I don't imagine Radley would be so thrilled about your upcoming marriage if you don't bring him the Davison fortune."

"Thank you," she said, nettled at his implication that without her "dowry" she would be a poor catch.

He grinned at her tone. "Come now, Philippa. If this was a love match you'd have brought him to your hideaway long ago... unless you've changed."

"I don't know what you're talking about," she said coldly. Conscious that her cheeks were growing pink, she rose from her seat and walked to the window.

"Then you've forgotten a great deal," he said, coming up behind her. "Perhaps I'd better remind you."

Within seconds he'd pulled her around and into his arms. The floor rocked beneath her at the feel of his mouth. His lips were firm and purposeful as he kissed her with a slow persuasiveness that carried a hint of threat. She'd been right to think of him as dangerous. There was danger in the hands that held her captive against him, and danger in the pressure of his body against the length of hers. Above all there was danger in her reactions, which seemed to riot out of control in the first instant. Before she had time to think she'd parted her lips, and he'd accepted the mute invitation, plunging his tongue into the moist warmth within.

He slid his arms around her, pressing her closer, and she responded wildly to the intimate contact. She wanted to enfold him between her thighs and draw him into herself until they melted into one. Corrado had gone straight to the heart of her desire, and there was no turning back.

He tore his mouth from hers, gasping slightly. "You haven't changed," he said thickly. "You're a passionate woman, Philippa. There are depths in you that Radley doesn't suspect."

The tip of his tongue flickered against her lips before she could answer, and she fought to hide the fevered tremors that went through her. There was no warmth in Corrado's eyes. He was a man in the grip of a physical appetite, but he hadn't surrendered to it. He was still wary, still mistrustful, watching her carefully to gauge her reaction.

Slowly she pulled away from him. She was trembling with shock and anger. "Why did you do that?" she demanded. "This is a business discussion. Nothing more. You had no right—"

"Didn't I?" he asked coolly. "I thought you understood how business was conducted. You've offered me a contract, and I have a right to read the small print before I reach a decision."

"The small print is in there," she said, flinging out a hand to the books.

"No, that's just the start. Your lips told me something I couldn't have discovered by asking. You're not in love with Radley, so there's nothing standing in the way of our marriage."

"Our *marriage*?" She was certain she'd misunderstood him.

"Marriage is the only logical way to handle this," he said coolly. "Inheritance taxes will take a chunk of your fortune. If you simply make me a gift of the rest there'll be even more. And finally, if there's any left after that it'll vanish as the shares crash in value."

"Why should they?"

"Because you can hardly make such a drastic change without an explanation. The market's bound to assume that the company's close to bankruptcy. But if we marry it can appear as a marriage settlement. There'll be no taxes and no questions."

"I said you've changed, but I had no idea how much," she said incredulously. "Once you were a decent man with a sense of honor. Now you're an unscrupulous rogue."

"And who made me one?" he demanded with the first flash of bitterness she'd seen in him. "Is it for you to lecture me about my methods? We have to be sensible about this."

"Oh, yes, let's be sensible," she said ironically. She was still reeling from the intensity of the pleasure she'd found in his arms, and her mind refused to accept that this conversation was taking place.

"You wanted to talk business," he reminded her, "and I'm offering you the only sensible business arrangement."

Once she'd longed to marry Corrado and had dreamed of how he might propose. Now he offered her a sensible business arrangement. Philippa drew a long, slow breath.

"Very well," she said quietly. "If it's the only sensible thing to do, we'll marry."

Twelve

Philippa came back to the present with a start and found she was shaking. The room had become suffocating, and she threw open the shutters to let the sunlight stream in. But no light could pierce the darkness of her memories. She'd discovered the secret from which Corrado's generosity had protected her. She knew now that it was she who had cheated him and ruined his life.

She'd given him her inheritance in the form of a marriage settlement and traveled to Italy to marry Corrado a month later. She'd eagerly looked forward to their meeting. The volcano she'd thought long dead had erupted without warning, and she was possessed by her newly awakened love. Though she knew Corrado didn't love her, she longed for some sign of warmth after the weeks apart.

But his manner had been gravely correct, even on the few occasions they'd been alone. He'd shown her over his home, and she'd ached to think how wonderful this might have been. How she would have loved to stand with him on the terrace as the sun set over Naples. How they could have laughed and kissed and crept away to be alone. Instead, the first evening had been spent signing more papers with his Italian lawyers.

He'd placed his car at her service, advising her to show Aunt Claire the locality as he'd be occupied with his factories for the next few days. She'd smiled mechanically and set out to behave like a blissful bride for her aunt's benefit, but all the time the pain in her heart had grown sharper.

There'd been the nightmare of the civil ceremony: herself and Corrado, side by side in the dark-paneled office at the town hall, Corrado signing the register with the same brisk efficiency he would have shown for any profitable contract.

She'd been determined to go through with the marriage, but her love had been like an open wound for which there was no balm. She'd endured the reception, smiling and laughing to cover the fact that her heart was breaking. Corrado behaved charmingly. No one could have guessed that he was marrying her to right a wrong, and that the shadow of twenty million pounds loomed over them. His eyes gave nothing away.

Once she'd slipped outside to be alone on the terrace and wonder at her own foolishness at ever thinking this could work. He'd come to find her, courteous and concerned, but reminding her that they had appearances to preserve. As she walked back into the house on his arm, Philippa had reflected despairingly that it would always be like this. Corrado would be a conscientious husband, but to the woman who loved him with all her heart and soul his conscientiousness would be a cruel mockery.

When she couldn't endure it any longer she'd escaped upstairs. She'd thought only of being alone and free of curious eyes, but once in her room she'd remembered the key to Corrado's car, still in her purse. It would be so easy to leave now and spare herself the anguish of the years ahead. A legal marriage had made the property his. Later there could be a divorce that left everything in his hands. Sadly she'd removed the wedding ring to which she'd pinned so many deluded hopes, and left the house unseen.

It was easy to take the car. Inside the house Don Ferrando had begun to sing. Some guests joined in a shouted chorus, and she started the engine under cover of the noise. A moment later she was on the road, and when she was clear of the house she'd stepped on the gas. She didn't know where she was going. She only knew she had to escape.

The road was poorly lit, and she was coming to a series of turns. She slowed, but not enough. A bend appeared swiftly out of the darkness. She swung into it too late and heard the crunching sound as the wheels hit the shoulder. The car seemed to jump, and then it was heading downward. In the glare of the headlights she saw the far bank of the ditch rushing up to meet her. Her head collided mercilessly with the steering wheel as the car came to an abrupt halt. She managed to climb out and back onto the road before oblivion descended on her.

That oblivion had separated her life into two distinct worlds. In one, Corrado had suggested marriage coolly and with no hint of love. In the other, she was his beloved, her heart warmed by his adoration, her body brought to glorious life by his passion.

Today the door between the two had opened. Somehow she must reconcile them and discover how the two Corrados could be the same man. She'd have no peace until she'd read the answer in his eyes.

She heard the screeching of car brakes outside. After a door slammed, there were running footsteps, then Corrado's voice filled with anguish calling her name.

Before she could answer the door of the hobby room was flung open, and he rushed in, his face pale. "Philippa!" he exclaimed. "Thank God." He pulled her into his arms and held her tightly. "Anna told me you reached the gate, but then turned and drove off." The arms holding her trembled, and she could feel the pounding of his heart against her own. "I was afraid," he said hoarsely. "It was so like last time when you left without warning—" He broke off and buried his mouth in her hair.

"God, I went crazy," he continued softly. "I even went back to the place where you had the accident. I thought perhaps you'd had some wild idea of recreating it. But there was no sign of you... and then I thought of this house. I always knew you'd come back here one day." He stopped abruptly and pushed her away from him so that he could look into her face.

"Philippa?" he said slowly, his tone asking the question he didn't dare voice.

"Yes." She nodded. "I came here to remember. And I have."

He watched her intently. "What...exactly have you remembered?"

"Everything. I know now that it was my fault. I ruined your life, Corrado."

"That isn't true," he said fiercely. "None of it was your fault. You were your father's innocent victim. And never say that you ruined my life. You *gave* me my life. But for you I'd have married the wrong woman, and then we'd never have found each other." He suddenly grew very still, his face fearful. "We *have* found each other...haven't we?" he asked. "Or...do you hate me, now that you know everything?"

"How could I ever hate you?" she cried passionately.

"If you knew how I've hated myself all these years. I was incapable of reason that day. Because I'd been hurt I lashed out at you unforgivably. You had acted in innocence, and afterward I was bitterly ashamed. I came back to ask your forgiveness, but it was too late. I wrote to you in England, but I guess your father took my letters."

"But I wrote to you, too, asking *your* forgiveness."

"I still have that letter. I've treasured it all these years. It was absolution for me, proof that you hadn't turned completely against me, and therefore I wasn't the wretched monster I felt myself to be. I answered it many times, but you never wrote again."

"I couldn't. When I didn't hear from you I thought you hadn't forgiven me."

"Oh, darling. I forgave you long ago. It was myself I couldn't forgive. You'd opened your heart to me so trustingly. For years I was haunted by the memory of you weeping, pleading with me, and my own harshness.

"I came to England as soon as I heard of your father's death. I longed to see you and ask if we could ever begin again. I had a shock when we met at the funeral. I'd known you as a tomboy, and I found a woman who was elegant and remote. But the remoteness vanished when you spoke to me, and I saw you'd grown into the warm, sweet person I'd always known you'd become. I realized why losing Maria hadn't hurt more, why I'd never loved anyone else since. I'd been waiting for you."

"You knew... then?" she asked breathlessly.

"I think I began to suspect years ago, when I had to tell Maria why we couldn't marry. I blamed your father, but I never mentioned you. Angry as I was, I instinctively protected you against her. It wasn't until much later that I understood why. My heart was drawn to you, and it was because *you* had seemed to betray me that I reacted so violently."

"But why didn't you just tell me all this when I came to your hotel after the funeral?"

"How could I? You were fabulously wealthy, and I had a claim on your guilt. If I'd told you how I felt I would have sounded like just another fortune hunter."

"Not to me," Philippa said at once. "Oh, Corrado, how little you knew me. My feelings never died. They only changed from adolescent infatuation into a woman's love. If you'd just reached out to me, shown me a little warmth, I'd have thrown myself into your arms."

"That's not how you seemed. You were so businesslike that I forced myself to be the same. When you offered me your inheritance I delayed my answer in order to be alone with you again. I was tormented with jealousy in case you loved Radley, but gradually I became sure you didn't.

"And then I had the idea of using your offer as a way of making you marry me. I went through that charade of examining the books, trying to pluck up courage for what I wanted to say. When I found that the firm really was under-performing I saw how I could suggest marriage as a business deal. I longed to tell you that it was only *you* I wanted, but I was afraid. I thought when you were my wife I could dare to show my love and try to win yours." His face broke into a smile of self-mockery. "Oh *piccina*, if you only knew how clever I thought I was being, how subtle..."

"And it was all needless," she told him tenderly. "I loved you so."

His face darkened. "Then why did you run from me on our wedding day?"

"*Because* I loved you and thought you didn't love me. I lost my nerve. I thought the civil ceremony would be enough to entitle you to the money, but I couldn't face years of a loveless marriage."

"It was agony when I found you gone—I thought I'd lost my chance to win you. But when you awoke with amnesia I realized that fate had given me a wonderful gift. While your mind was blank you were free from the past, of your sense of guilt. I hoped that I could win you for love alone. That's why I kept the truth from you. It was wrong of me, but I warned you once that I wasn't terribly scrupulous in my methods, and now you see it's true."

He lowered his mouth to hers, and for a long time they were silent. It was the first kiss of their true love, when they could see each other clearly at last. "You should have trusted me," she told him as he released her. "I trusted you."

"I told myself I was protecting you for your sake, but the fact is that I was a coward. I'd found the one woman in the world that I could love, but you'd already run away on our wedding day. I was afraid if I told you everything you'd leave again, and I knew I couldn't bear that. So I kept putting off the moment to give myself more time to win your heart.

"I began to see how stupid I'd been when Michael Radley was here, and you showed your faith in me. It was the most wonderful moment of my life, but it made me ashamed, remembering how cruelly I'd once treated you."

"So that's why you looked so strange? I wondered if you were still hiding something."

"I was, because even then I couldn't bear to tell you how you'd been involved in your father's actions. But last night I took out the letter you wrote me years ago and read it again. It didn't contain a single word of blame for the brutal way I'd behaved, and I saw that your generosity then was the same generosity you showed me when Radley was here. The sweet girl of those days had grown into the woman who loved me, who could understand and forgive. Your love and faith gave me the courage to face you. If this hadn't happened, I was going to tell you everything tonight."

He drew her close again, and they clung together, not kissing, but drawing strength from each other's presence. At last he said, "Now that there are no more secrets between us, I want you to cancel that marriage settlement. I never meant to take anything from you." He took her face between his hands. "I love you so much. If I have your heart, that's all the wealth I want."

He'd told her before that he loved her, but it was as though she were hearing it for the first time. She knew now that she'd been right to believe in him and trust him.

"You've always had my heart," she said, smiling tenderly. "You won it when I was ten years old and you came into my father's office on your first day at work. I went home and wrote in my diary, 'When I grow up I'm going to marry Corrado.'" They laughed together, and she added, "Darling, keep the money. It's yours by right. You don't have to convince me that you married me for love."

"I don't want your money, *piccina*," he said firmly. "I can make my own."

"Well, I don't want it either. The firm deserves to be in your hands, and we'll put the income in trust for our children."

Something in her tone made him look at her with eager hope. "Children?"

"You were wrong about there being no more secrets between us. There's still one that I've been longing to tell you."

"Philippa—"

She took his hand. "Not here. Let's talk about it on the way home."

He followed her lead out into the sun, leaving the past without a backward glance. The shadows had finally dispersed, and the way ahead was flooded with glowing light.

* * * * *

Silhouette Desire

COMING NEXT MONTH

#421 LOVE POTION—Jennifer Greene
Dr. Grey Treveran didn't believe in magic until he was rescued by the bewitching Jill Stanton. She taught him how to dream again, and he taught her how to love.

#422 ABOUT LAST NIGHT...—Nancy Gramm
Enterprising Kate Connors only had one obstacle in the way of her cleanup campaign—Mitch Blake. Then their heated battle gave way to passion....

#423 HONEYMOON HOTEL—Sally Goldenbaum
Sydney Hanover needed a million dollars in thirty days to save Candlewick Inn. She tried to tell herself that Brian Hennesy was foe, not friend, but her heart wouldn't listen.

#424 FIT TO BE TIED—Joan Johnston
Jennifer Smith and Matthew Benson were tied together to prove a point, but before their thirty days were up, Matthew found himself wishing their temporary ties were anything but!

#425 A PLACE IN YOUR HEART—Amanda Lee
Jordan Callahan was keeping a secret from Lisa Patterson. He wanted more than their past friendship now, but could the truth destroy his dreams?

#426 TOGETHER AGAIN—Ariel Berk
Six years before, past events had driven Keith LaMotte and Annie Jameson apart. They'd both made mistakes; now they had to forgive each other before they could be... together again.

AVAILABLE NOW:

#415 FEVER
Elizabeth Lowell

#416 FOR LOVE ALONE
Lucy Gordon

#417 UNDER COVER
Donna Carlisle

#418 NO TURNING BACK
Christine Rimmer

#419 THE SECOND MR. SULLIVAN
Elaine Camp

#420 ENAMORED
Diana Palmer

Silhouette Special Edition
NORA ROBERTS'S 50TH SILHOUETTE NOVEL